THE PRESCHOOL TEACHER'S PET

Time-Savers for All Reasons & Seasons

Written by Linda Schwartz
Illustrated by Beverly Armstrong

The Learning Works

The purchase of this book entitles the individual teacher to reproduce copies for use in the classroom.

The reproduction of any part for an entire school or school system or for commercial use is strictly prohibited.

No form of this work may be reproduced or transmitted or recorded without written permission from the publisher.

Copyright © 1989
THE LEARNING WORKS, INC.
P.O. Box 6187
Santa Barbara, CA 93160
All rights reserved.
Printed in the United States of America

Introduction

The Preschool Teacher's Pet is a time-saving collection of ready-to-use

- activities
- alphabet charts
- announcements
- awards
- birthday notes
- borders
- calendars
- charts
- clip art
- counting activities
- facts
- forms
- get-well notes
- holiday suggestions
- invitations
- letters
- memos
- miscellaneous information
- name tags
- number activities
- readiness activities
- worksheets

Compiled by a former classroom teacher, these materials cover the basic preschool readiness skills such as classifying, matching, developing small motor skills, perception, rhyming, and sequencing. Also included are activities to teach the alphabet, counting, and the numbers one through ten. They have been selected for you, for your students, and for the aides, parents, substitutes, and others who work with you in educating preschool children.

The pages in this book will help you get organized, get acquainted with your preschoolers, keep track of their progress, give encouragement, recognize achievement, fill empty hours on rainy days, and communicate effectively with aides, substitute teachers, and parents—even when there isn't time!

But teaching and learning should not be all forms and facts. There's got to be some fun. Border patterns will help you decorate bulletin boards and walls. Clip art cutouts will make it easy for you to add a touch of whimsy to worksheets you create and to the announcements and letters you send home.

The Preschool Teacher's Pet doesn't teach. Only you can do that. But its pages are packed with possibilities—ways to make teaching easier for you and learning more fun for your children. It's all of the many facts, forms, and ideas you need in one single, convenient package.

Contents

Forms and Notes 7-34

Forms for Teachers 8-12
Birthday Boxes 8
All-Purpose Chart 9
Any Month Calendar 10
Things to Do Today 11
Handy Home Information 12

Forms for Parents 13-18
A Call for Supplies 13
Portrait of Our Preschool Day 14
All About Classwork 15
Classwork 16
Help Wanted 17
Our Preschool Newsletter 18

**Forms for Substitutes
and Aides** 19-25
Helpful Hints for Aides
  and Substitutes 19
Class List 20
Lesson Plans for My Substitute 21
Aide Assignment Sheet:
  Working with Students 22
Aide Assignment Sheet:
  Clerical Duties 23
Activity Evaluation Sheet for Aides . 24
Aide Awards 25

Name Tags and Notes 26-34
Name Tags 26
General Notes 27-28
Reminders 29
Announcements 30
Invitations 31
Thank-You Notes 32
Get-Well Notes 33
Happy Birthday Notes 34

Awards 35-46
All-Purpose Awards 36
Effort and Improvement Awards 37
Good Friend and Curiosity Awards ... 38
Listening and Following
  Directions Awards 39
Behavior and Sportsmanship
  Awards 40
Art and Creativity Awards 41
Community Helper and
  Science Awards 42
Alphabet Awards 43
Number and Counting Awards 44
Color and Shape Awards 45
"I Know" Awards 46

The Preschool Teacher's Pet
©1989–The Learning Works, Inc.

Contents
(continued)

Art and Holiday Happenings . . 47-90

Multipurpose Worksheets 48-57
September 48
October 49
November 50
December 51
January 52
February 53
March 54
April 55
May 56
June 57

Clip Art 58-79
Clip Art 58
Farm Animals 59
Wild Animals 60
Water Animals 61
Pets 62
Prehistoric Creatures 63
Plant Life 64
Things to Eat 65
More Things to Eat 66
Toys and Games 67
Art, Music, and Drama 68
Holidays and Seasons–Fall 69
Holidays and Seasons–Winter 70
Holidays and Seasons–
    Spring and Summer 71
Transportation 72

Clip Art (con't)
Community Helpers 73-78
Space Race 79

Borders 80-90
Borders 80
September: Squirrels and Leaves 81
October: Pumpkins and Ghosts 82
November: Turkeys and Corn 83
December: Bells and Bows 84
January: Snowmen and Hats 85
February: Hatchets and Hearts 86
March: Shamrocks and Tulips 87
April: Ducks and Bunnies 88
May: Daisies and Suns 89
General: Dancers and Hands 90

Numbers and Counting 91-112
Numbers 1-10 92-101
Counting 1-10 102-112

The Alphabet 113-140
Letters of the Alphabet 114-139
Alphabet Chart 140

Reading Readiness 141-192
Sequencing 142-149
Classifying 150-157
Perception 158-165
Matching 166-173
Rhyming 174-181
Motor Skills 182-192

Forms & Notes

Forms and Notes
Forms for Teachers

Birthday Boxes

Write each child's name, birthdate, and age in the appropriate place. Then keep this sheet for reference.

Preschool Teacher's Pet
89—The Learning Works, Inc.

Forms and Notes
Forms for Teachers

All-Purpose Chart

1																
2																
3																
4																
5																
6																
7																
8																
9																
10																
11																
12																
13																
14																
15																
16																
17																
18																
19																
20																
21																
22																
23																
24																
25																
26																
27																
28																
29																
30																

The Preschool Teacher's Pet
©1989–The Learning Works, Inc.

Forms and Notes
Forms for Teachers

Any Month Calendar

SUNDAY	MONDAY	TUESDAY	WEDNESDAY	THURSDAY	FRIDAY	SATURDAY

Forms and Notes
Forms for Teachers

Things to Do Today

Check when done.

Forms and Notes
Forms for Teachers

Handy Home Information

	Name	Address	Telephone
1			
2			
3			
4			
5			
6			
7			
8			
9			
10			
11			
12			
13			
14			
15			
16			
17			
18			
19			
20			
21			
22			
23			
24			
25			

The Preschool Teacher's Pet
©1989–The Learning Works, Inc.

A Call for Supplies

Dear Parents,

This year our preschool will be involved in many exciting projects. We need your help in gathering the supplies and materials that will be used throughout the year in our crafts center. Please help us by sending to school any of the following materials that you would like to donate:

- buttons
- cans
- cardboard tubes
- egg cartons
- fabric scraps
- magazines
- margarine tubs
- milk cartons
- pipe cleaners
- plastic containers of various sizes
- ribbon
- wallpaper scraps
- wire hangers
- wrapping paper
- yarn

Thank you for your help.

Sincerely,

_____

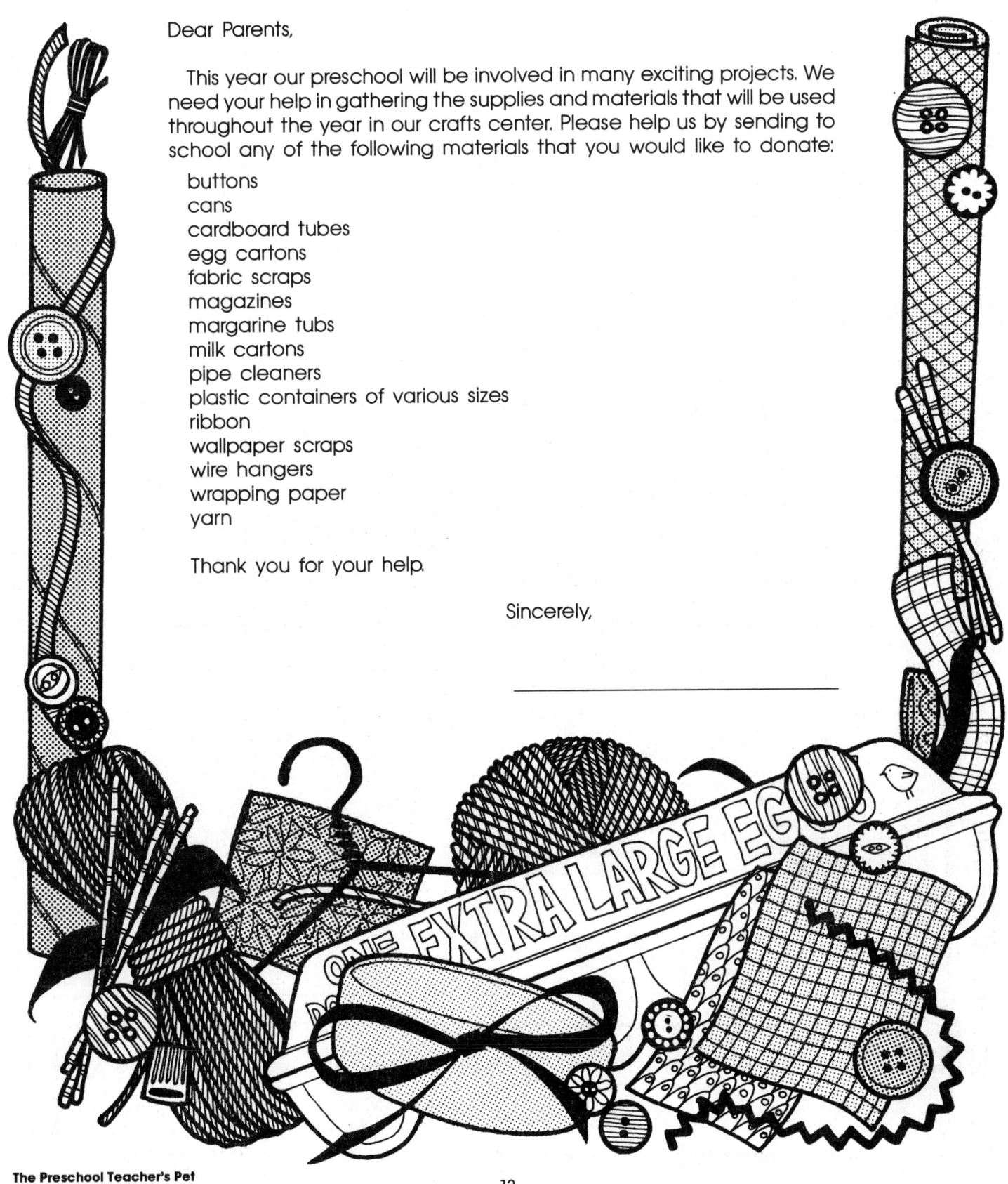

Forms and Notes
Forms for Parents

Portrait of Our Preschool Day

Dear Parents,

   We hope you will come and visit our preschool classroom. Here's a copy of our daily schedule to help you plan your visit.

   Sincerely,

   _____

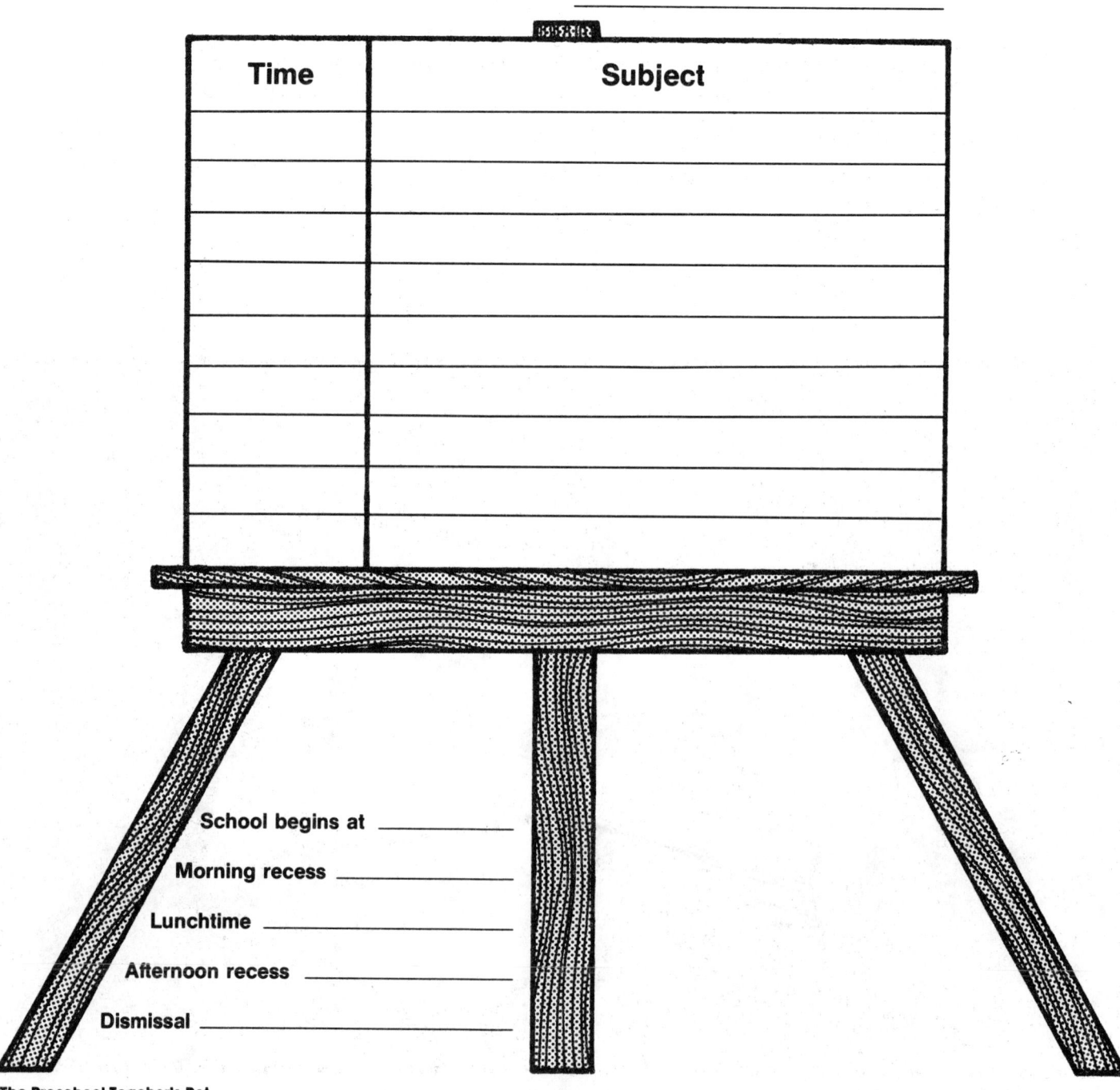

Time	Subject

School begins at _____
Morning recess _____
Lunchtime _____
Afternoon recess _____
Dismissal _____

All About Classwork

Dear Parents,

Communication between home and preschool is vital to your child's success in the classroom.

To keep you informed and aware of what we are doing, I plan to send home a folder with papers your child has completed every

_____.

Please take the time to review and discuss these papers with your child. Then date and initial the form on your child's folder, keep the papers (unless otherwise noted), and have your child return the empty folder to me within two days.

Your cooperation is greatly appreciated.

Sincerely,

_____.

Classwork

Dear Parents,

Inside this folder/envelope are _____ papers for the week. Please take time to review and discuss them with your child. Then date and sign this form and have your child return the empty folder to me by _____ of each week.

Date	Parent's Signature	Parent's Comments

Forms and Notes
Forms for Parents

Help Wanted

Dear Parents,

We will be involved in a variety of projects in preschool this year and would appreciate your help. Please take time to fill out the attached form and have your child return it to me as soon as possible.

Sincerely,

_____

Name _____
Address _____
Phone _____

1. I am willing to help in the following areas:
   - ☐ phone committee
   - ☐ sewing
   - ☐ cooking
   - ☐ carpentry
   - ☐ drama
   - ☐ music
   - ☐ dancing
   - ☐ arts and crafts
   - ☐ field trips
   - ☐ _____
   - ☐ _____
   - ☐ _____
   - ☐ _____
   - ☐ _____
   - ☐ _____
   - ☐ _____
   - ☐ _____
   - ☐ _____

2. I would enjoy
   - ☐ working with individual students
   - ☐ working with small groups
   - ☐ duplicating worksheets
   - ☐ preparing learning centers
   - ☐ making games
   - ☐ typing
   - ☐ performing other clerical tasks
   - ☐ _____
   - ☐ _____
   - ☐ _____

3. I have the following special interest, talent, hobby, or occupation I would be willing to share with the class:

   _____

4. The best times for me to help in the class are on
   - ☐ Monday ☐ Tuesday ☐ Wednesday ☐ Thursday ☐ Friday

   at _____ o'clock or _____.

Forms and Notes
Forms for Parents

Our Preschool Newsletter

Date: _____   Issue Number: _____

What We're Learning

Suggestions for Parents

Dates to Save

A Classroom Original
(poem, art, or quote)

Forms and Notes
Forms for Substitutes and Aides

Helpful Hints
For Aides and Substitutes

1. A teacher who can help you is _____.

2. Classroom aides or volunteers who are scheduled to come in today are

Name	Time	Assignment
_____	_____	_____
_____	_____	_____

3. You will find the following essential items in the places indicated.
   Lesson plans _____
   Seating chart _____
   Teacher's manuals _____

4. My usual roll-call procedure is _____
   _____

5. The students on medication are _____
   _____

6. Emergency procedures are as follows: _____
   _____
   _____

7. Other: _____
   _____
   _____

The Preschool Teacher's Pet
©1989–The Learning Works, Inc.

Forms and Notes
Forms for Substitutes and Aides

Class List

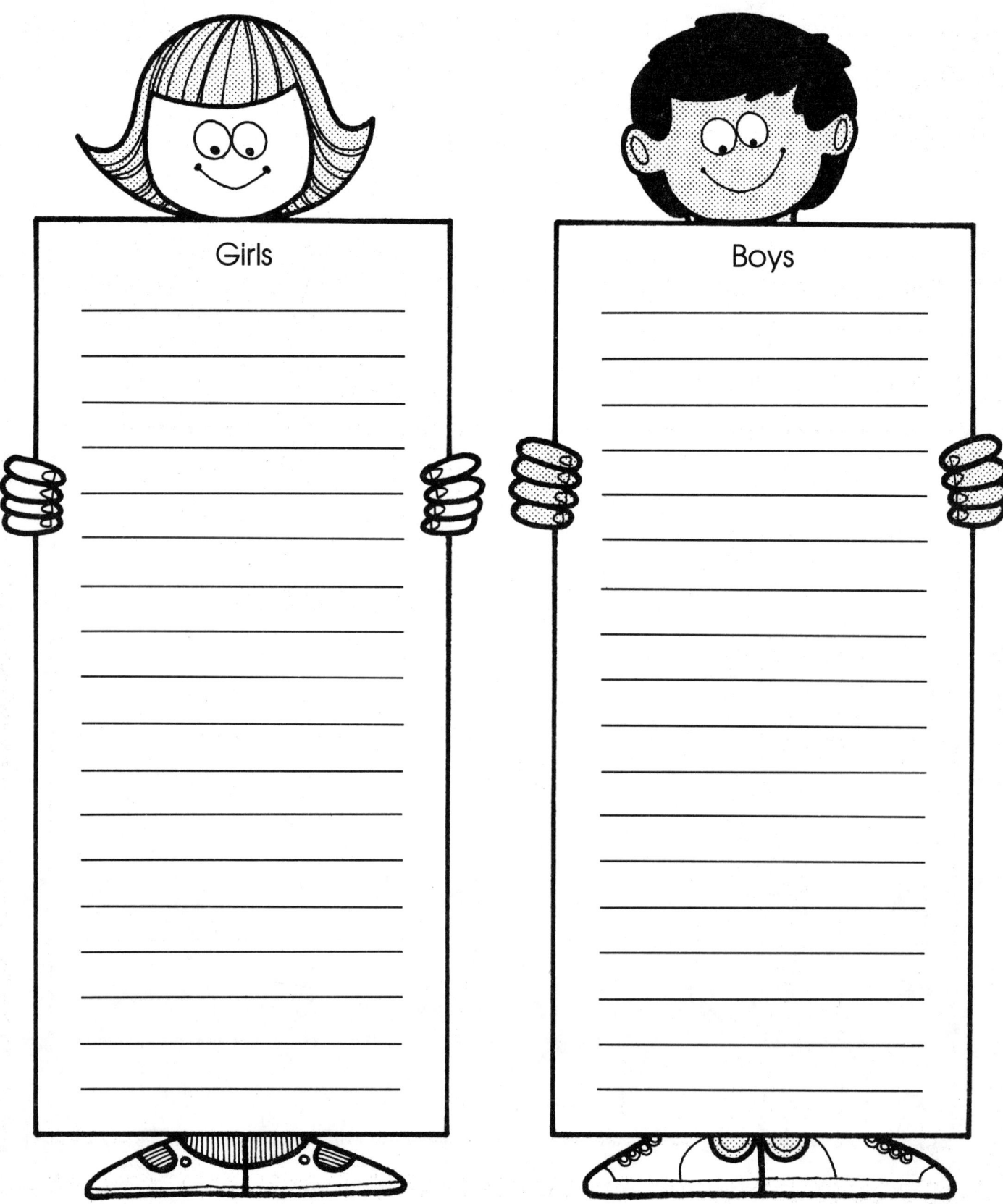

Forms and Notes
Forms for Substitutes and Aides

Lesson Plans For My Substitute

Daily Schedule
Class Begins _____
Morning Recess _____
Lunch _____
Afternoon Recess _____
Dismissal _____

Date _____

Time	Subject	Description

The Preschool Teacher's Pet
©1989–The Learning Works, Inc.

Forms and Notes
Forms for Substitutes and Aides

Aide Assignment Sheet
Working with Students

Name _____   Date _____

Activity	Student(s) Involved	Comments
☐ Language		
☐ Math		
☐ Music / Art		
☐ Assist with the following learning center activity:		
☐ Assist the following group:		
☐ Other		

Forms and Notes
Forms for Substitutes and Aides

Aide Assignment Sheet
Clerical Duties

Name_____ Date_____

Activity	Special Instructions	Needed By
☐ Type ditto masters	☐ of pages _____ in _____ ☐ of the attached sheets	
☐ Make a thermofax master	☐ of pages _____ in _____ ☐ of the attached sheets	
☐ Alphabetize		
☐ File		
☐ Run copies of _____	Number of copies needed _____ Print ☐ on one side ☐ on two sides	
☐ Grade the attached papers		
☐ Make the described game or activity		
☐ Cut paper	Type of paper _____ Color(s) _____ Number of sheets _____ Dimensions _____	
☐ Design a calendar for the month of _____	Suggested picture or theme _____ _____ _____	
☐ Design a bulletin board	Subject _____ Theme _____ Purpose _____	

Forms and Notes
Forms for Substitutes and Aides

Activity Evaluation Sheet
For Aides

Name _____ Date _____

Assignment _____

To help me evaluate the effectiveness of the activity you supervised, please fill out this sheet and return it to me.

1. I felt that the activity was
   - ☐ very effective
   - ☐ satisfactory
   - ☐ ineffective because _____
   _____
   _____

2. The following students had difficulty with the activity:
   _____
   _____

3. The behavior of the following students was a problem:
   _____
   _____

4. If the activity is done again, I would suggest that the following changes be made:
   _____
   _____
   _____

5. Additional comments or suggestions: _____
   _____
   _____
   _____

Forms and Notes
Forms for Substitutes and Aides

Aide Awards

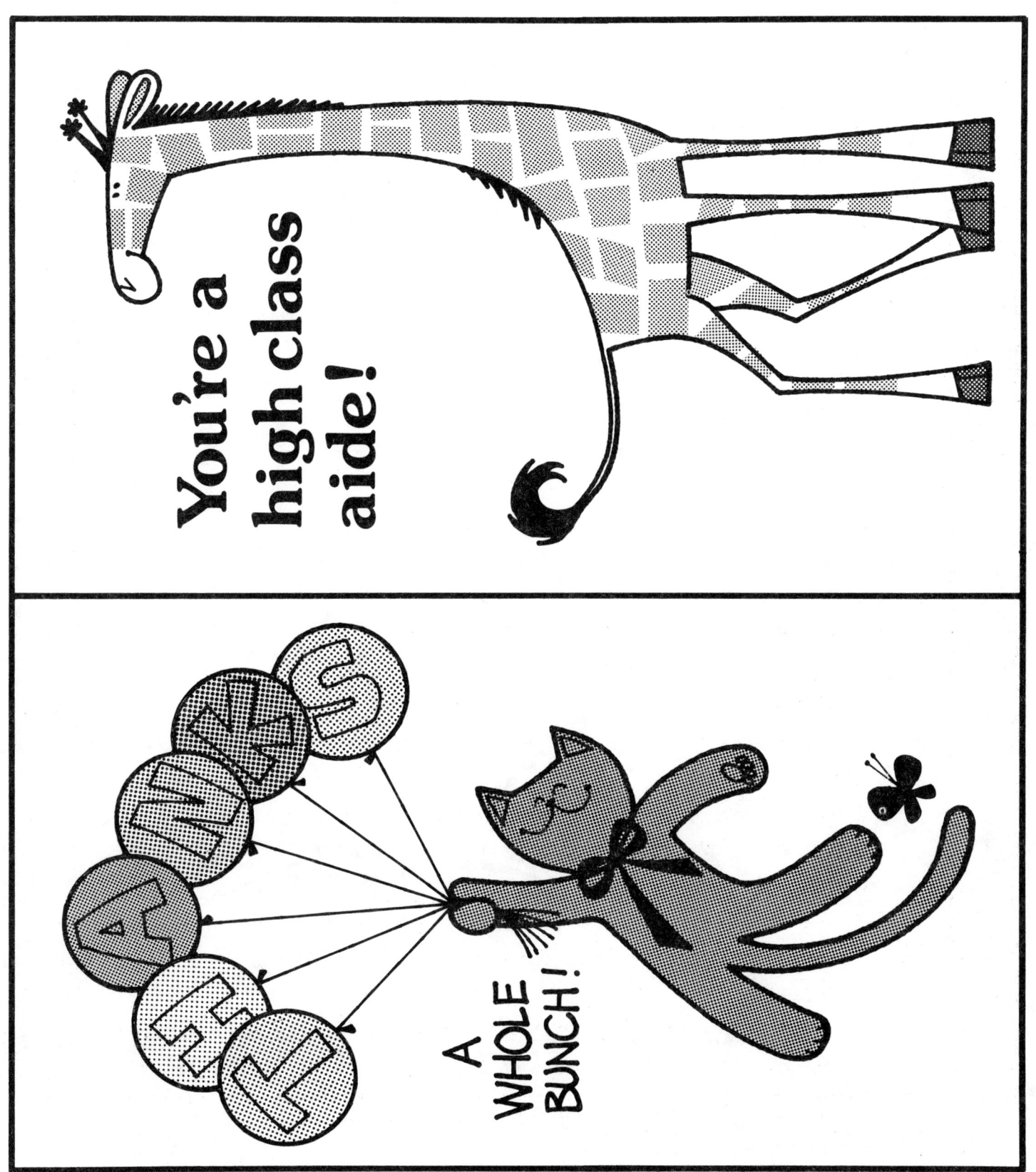

Name Tags

These all-purpose name tags are ideal for use by substitutes, visitors, and guest speakers and for use on field trips, at open house, and on many other occasions.

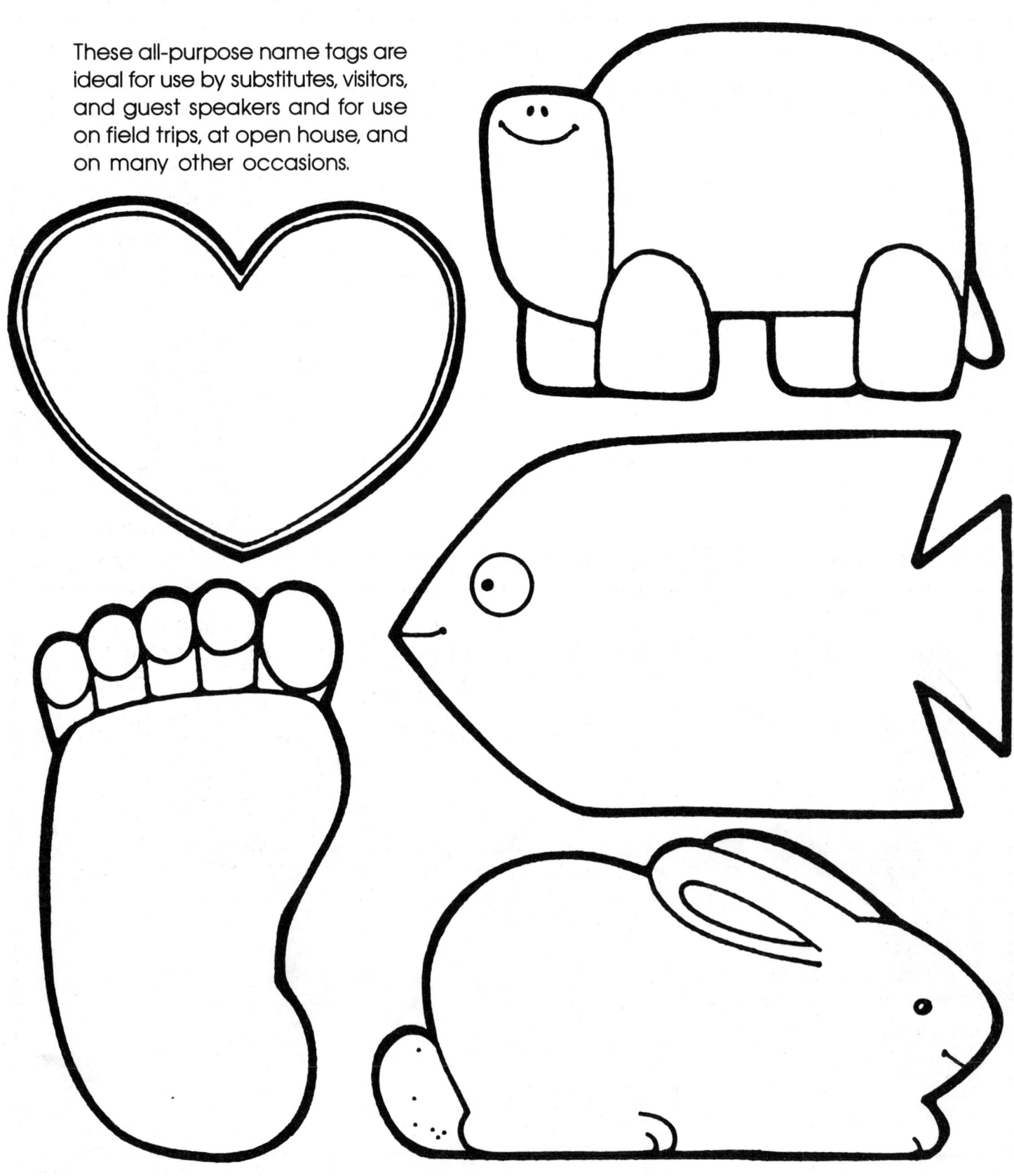

Forms and Notes
Name Tags and Notes

General Notes

CLASSROOM CALENDAR

TEACHER TALK

from the teacher's desk

General Notes
(continued)

teacher talk

from the teacher

Reminders

Don't forget!

Remember

Announcements

A FLYER TO PARENTS

ANNOUNCING...

Forms and Notes
Name Tags and Notes

Invitations

Forms and Notes
Name Tags and Notes

Thank-You Notes

Thanks for all your help!

MOOOCHAS GRACIAS

TO _____
FROM _____
FOR _____
_____

Get-Well Notes

Forms and Notes
Name Tags and Notes

Happy Birthday Notes

Awards

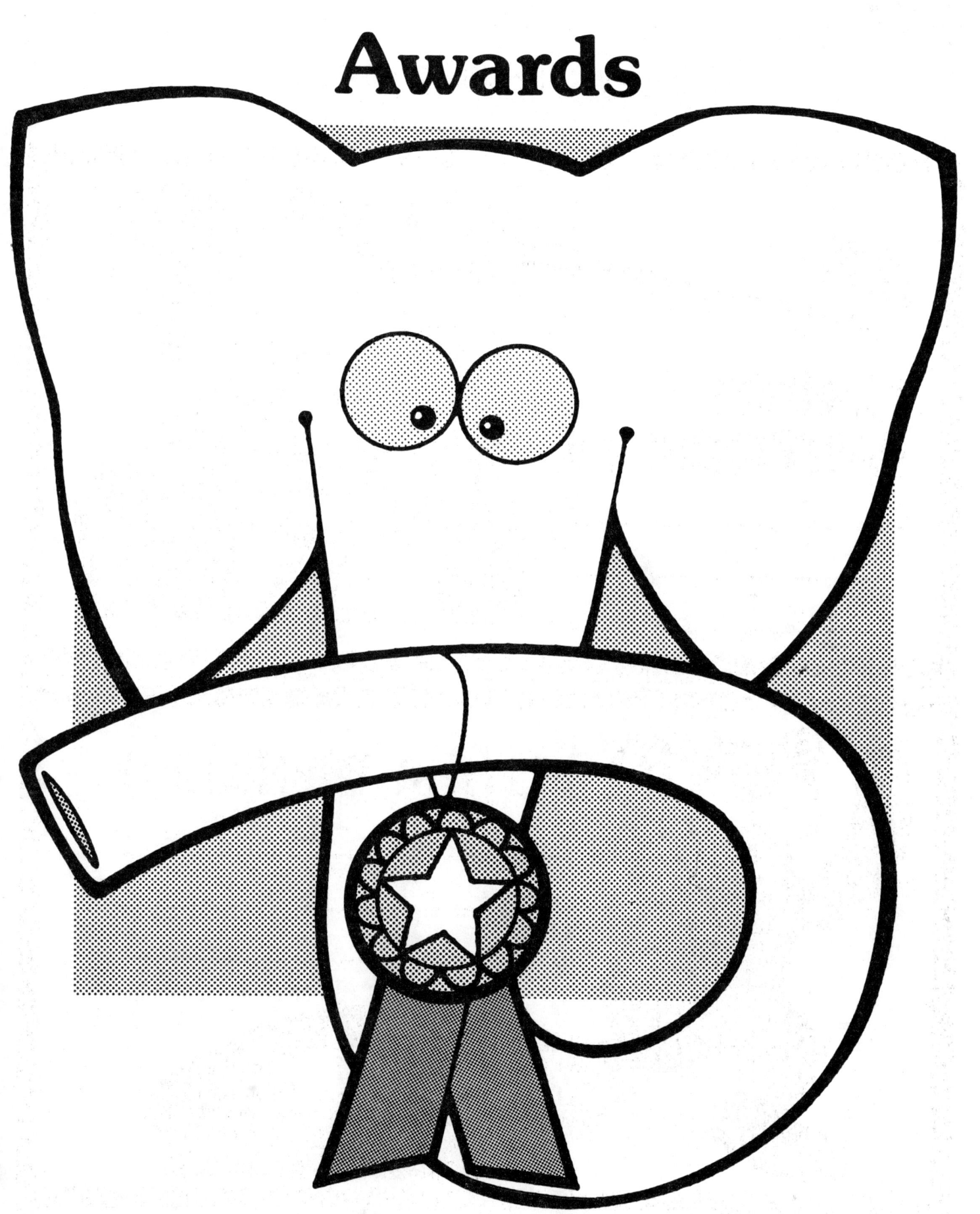

Awards

I AM A SUPER KID!

To _____
For _____
_____
_____
(signature)
(date)

You're terrific!

To _____
For _____
_____
_____
(signature)
(date)

The Preschool Teacher's Pet
©1989–The Learning Works, Inc.

36

ENORMOUS EFFORT AWARD

To _____
For _____ Date _____

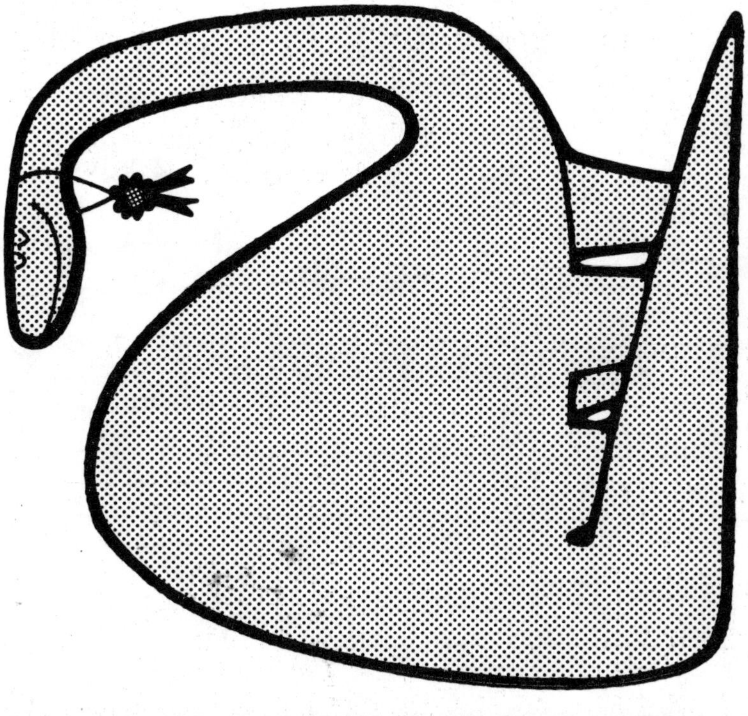

YOU'RE SHOWING BIG IMPROVEMENT!

To _____
For _____

(signature) _____
(date) _____

Awards

GOOD FRIEND AWARD

CERTIFICATE OF CURIOSITY

To _____
For _____
Signature _____
    Date _____

Awards

_____ (name)

CAN FOLLOW DIRECTIONS, AND I'M GLAD!

_____ (signature)
_____ (date)

SUPER LISTENER

To _____
From _____
Date _____

The Preschool Teacher's Pet
©1989–The Learning Works, Inc.

Awards

GREAT BEHAVIOR AWARD

To _____
For _____
From _____
Date _____

GOOD SPORT CERTIFICATE

To _____
For _____
From _____ Date _____

The Preschool Teacher's Pet
©1989–The Learning Works, Inc.

Awards

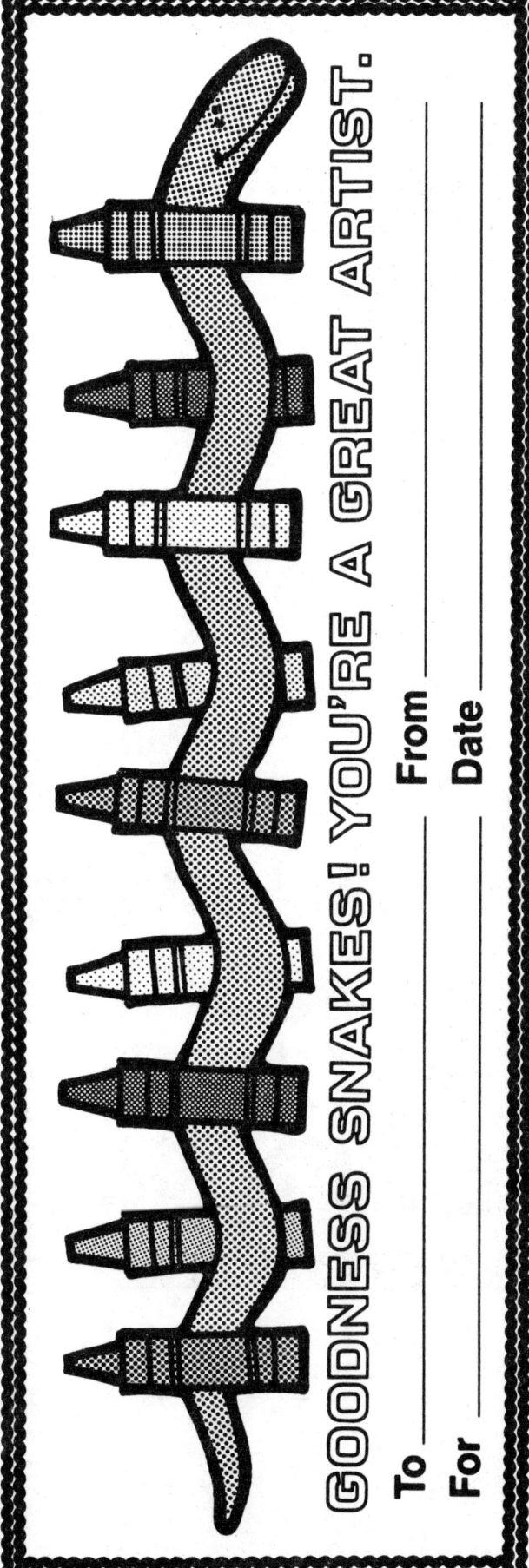

GOODNESS SNAKES! YOU'RE A GREAT ARTIST.

To _____
For _____
From _____
Date _____

CREATIVE KID CERTIFICATE

Given to _____
For _____
By _____
(signature)
On _____
(date)

The Preschool Teacher's Pet
©1989–The Learning Works, Inc.

Awards

COMMUNITY HELPER EXPERT

To _____
For _____
_____
From _____
Date _____

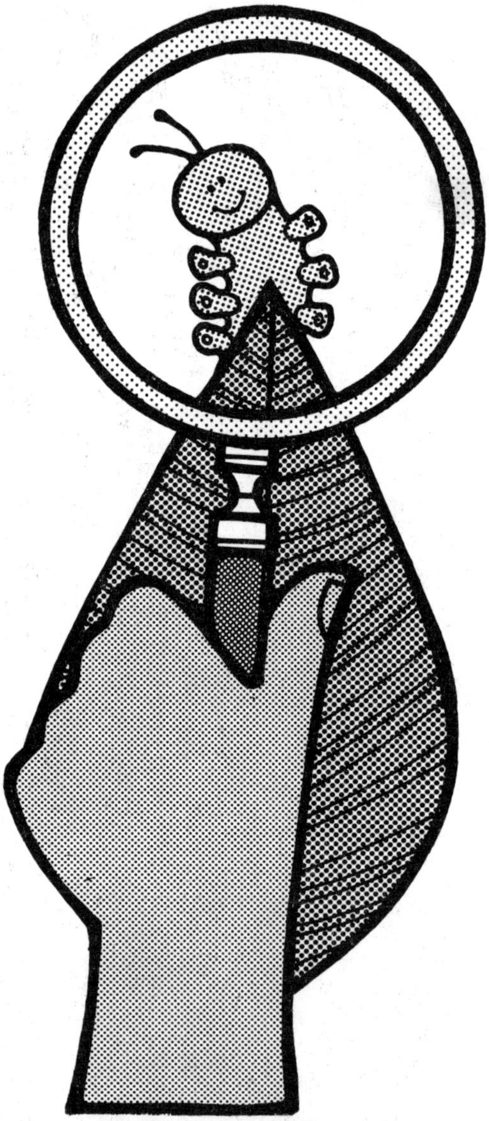

SUPER SCIENTIST

To _____
For _____
_____
From _____
Date _____

The Preschool Teacher's Pet
©1989–The Learning Works, Inc.

Awards

_____
knows all about the alphabet!

_____
teacher

_____
date

_____
can recite the alphabet!

_____
teacher

_____
date

Awards

_____
can count to
_____

_____
teacher

_____
date

_____
knows about numbers.

_____
teacher

_____
date

Awards

_____
knows the colors!

_____ _____
teacher   date

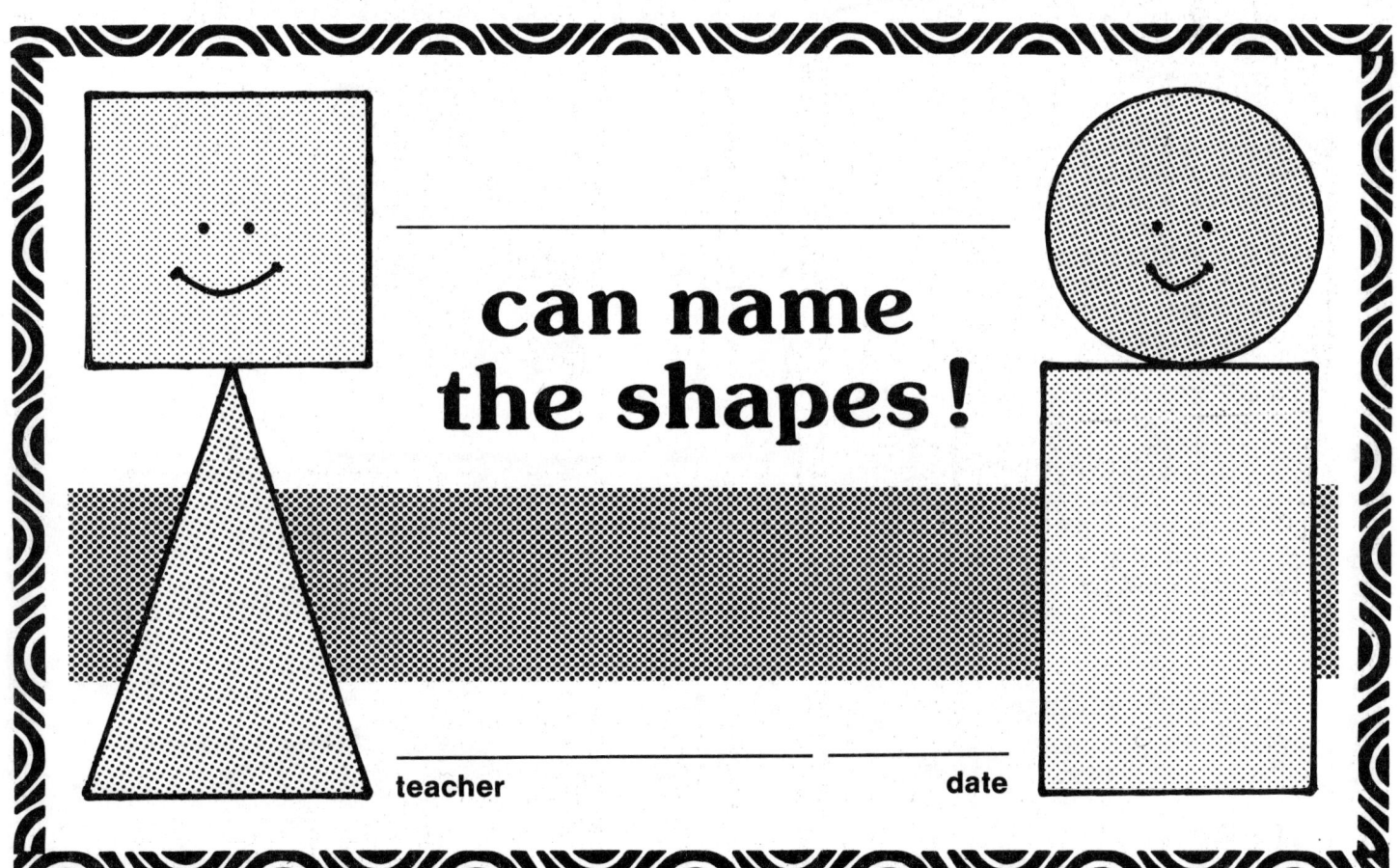
_____
can name the shapes!

_____ _____
teacher   date

Awards

I know my address!

_____
name

_____
date

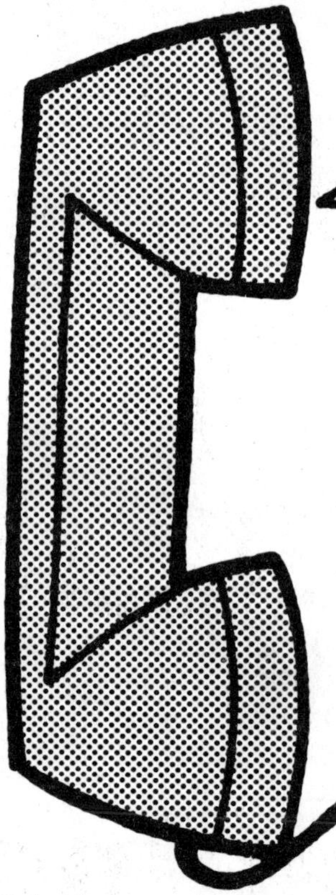

I know my telephone number!

_____
name

_____
date

Art & Holiday Happenings

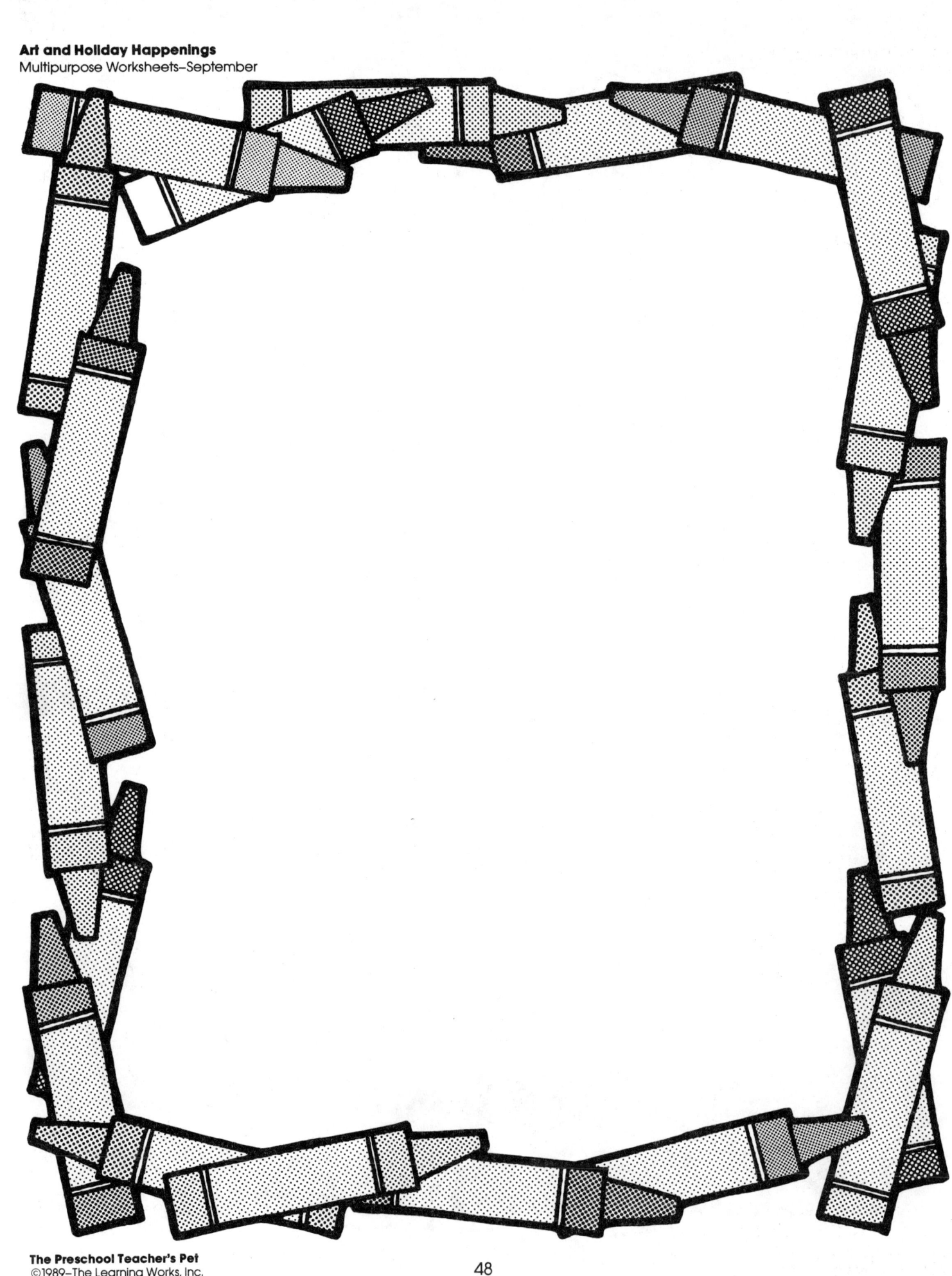

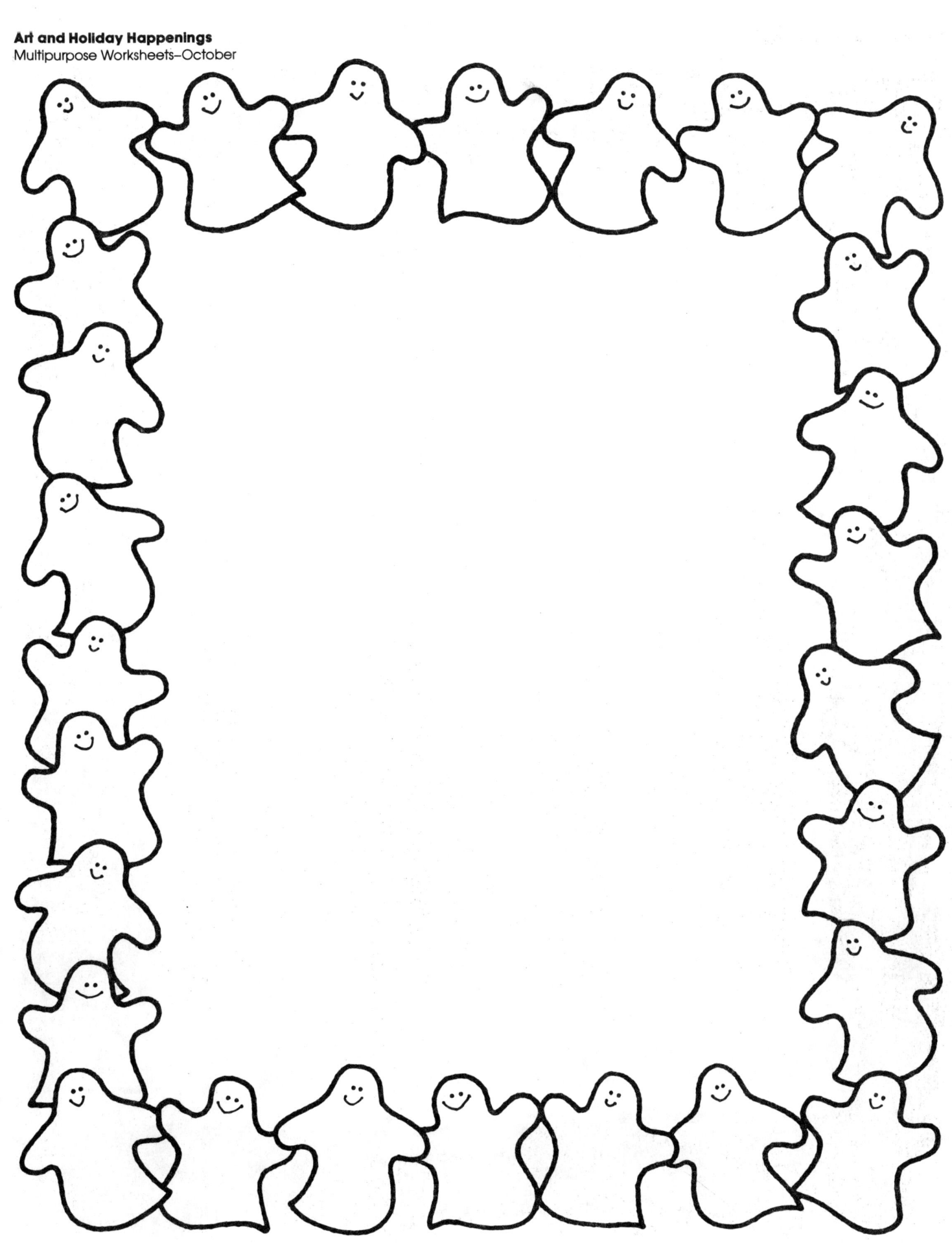

Art and Holiday Happenings
Multipurpose Worksheets–November

Art and Holiday Happenings
Multipurpose Worksheets–December

Art and Holiday Happenings
Multipurpose Worksheets–January

Art and Holiday Happenings
Multipurpose Worksheets–February

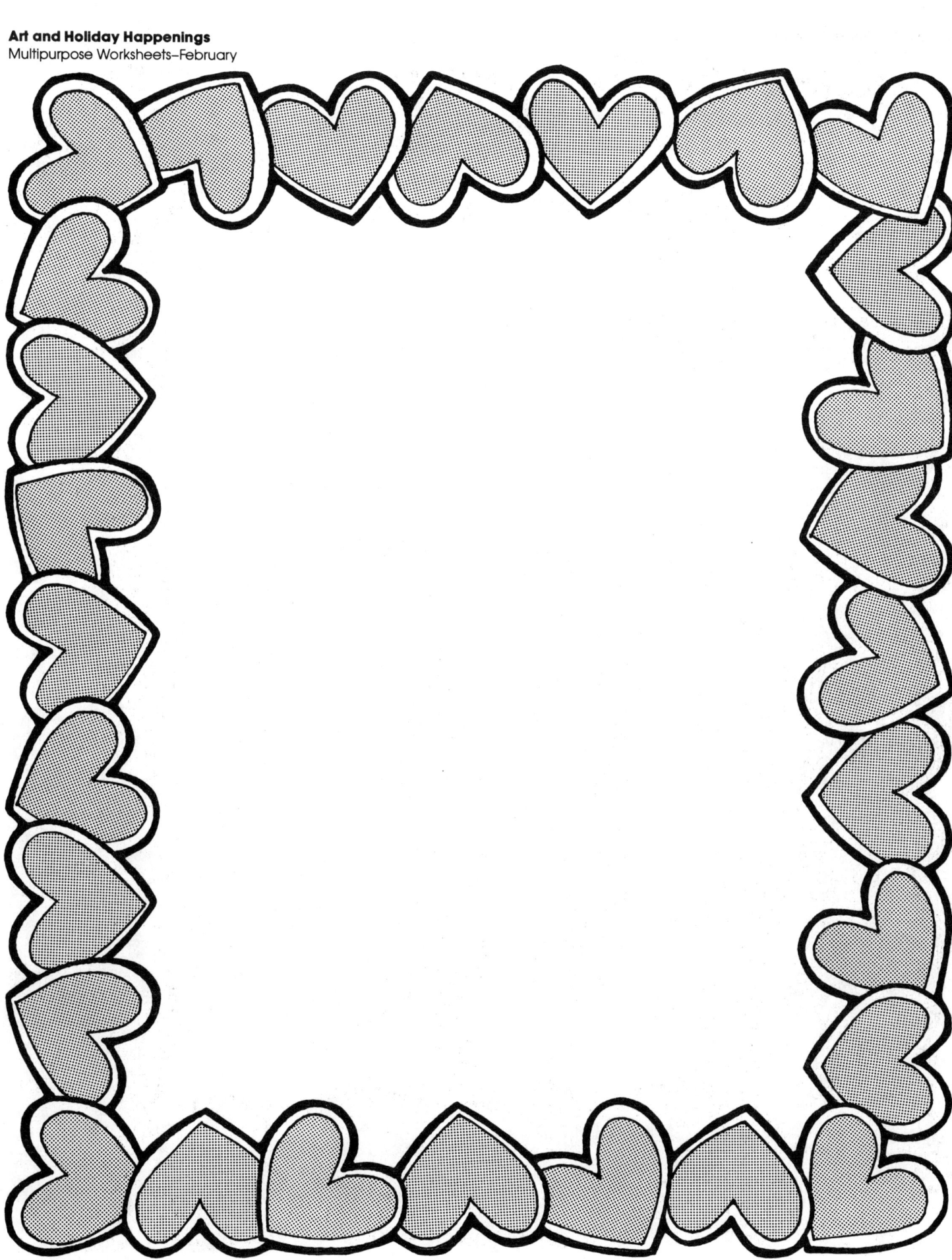

The Preschool Teacher's Pet
©1989–The Learning Works, Inc.

Art and Holiday Happenings
Multipurpose Worksheets—March

Art and Holiday Happenings
Multipurpose Worksheets–April

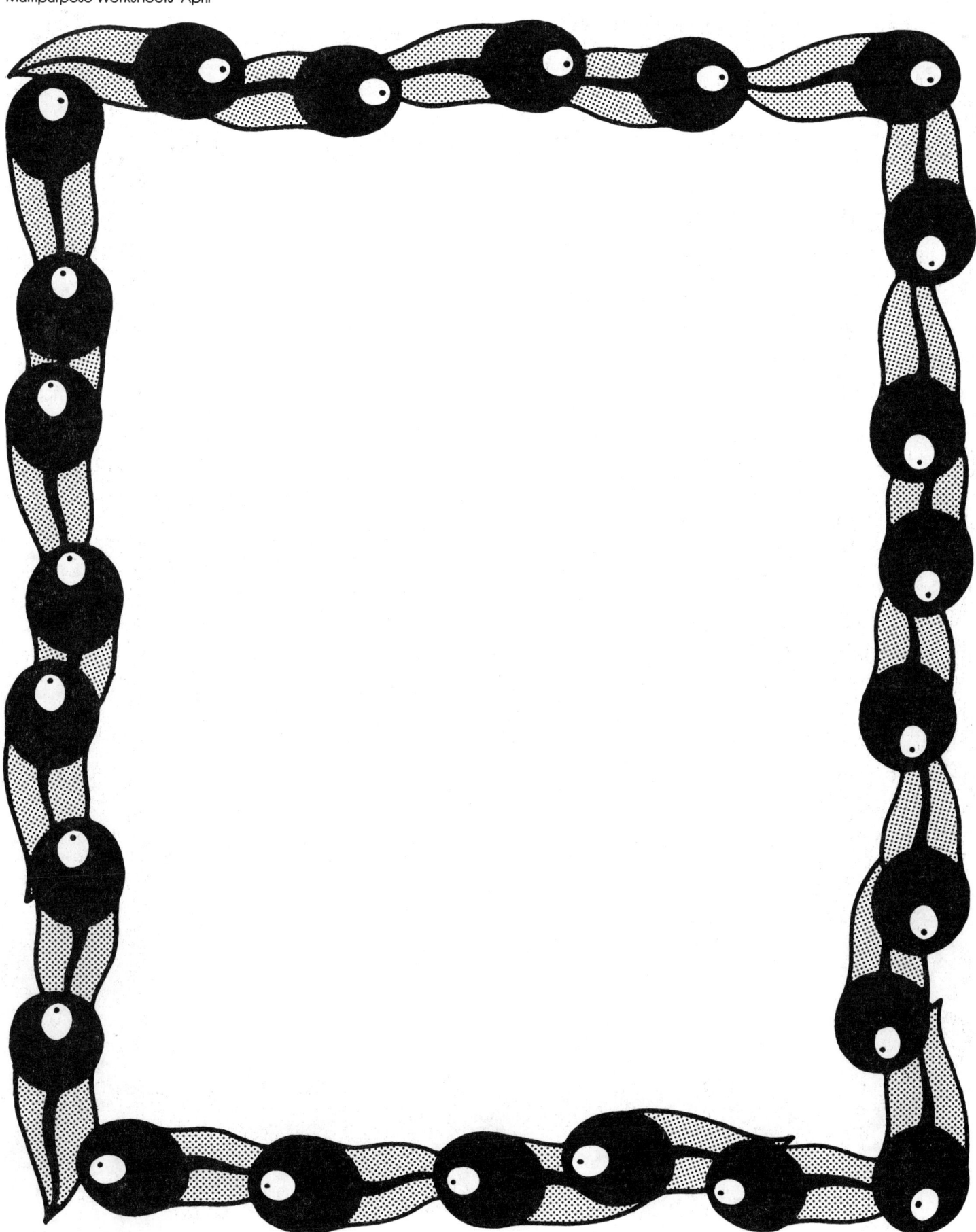

Art and Holiday Happenings
Multipurpose Worksheets—May

Art and Holiday Happenings
Multipurpose Worksheets–June

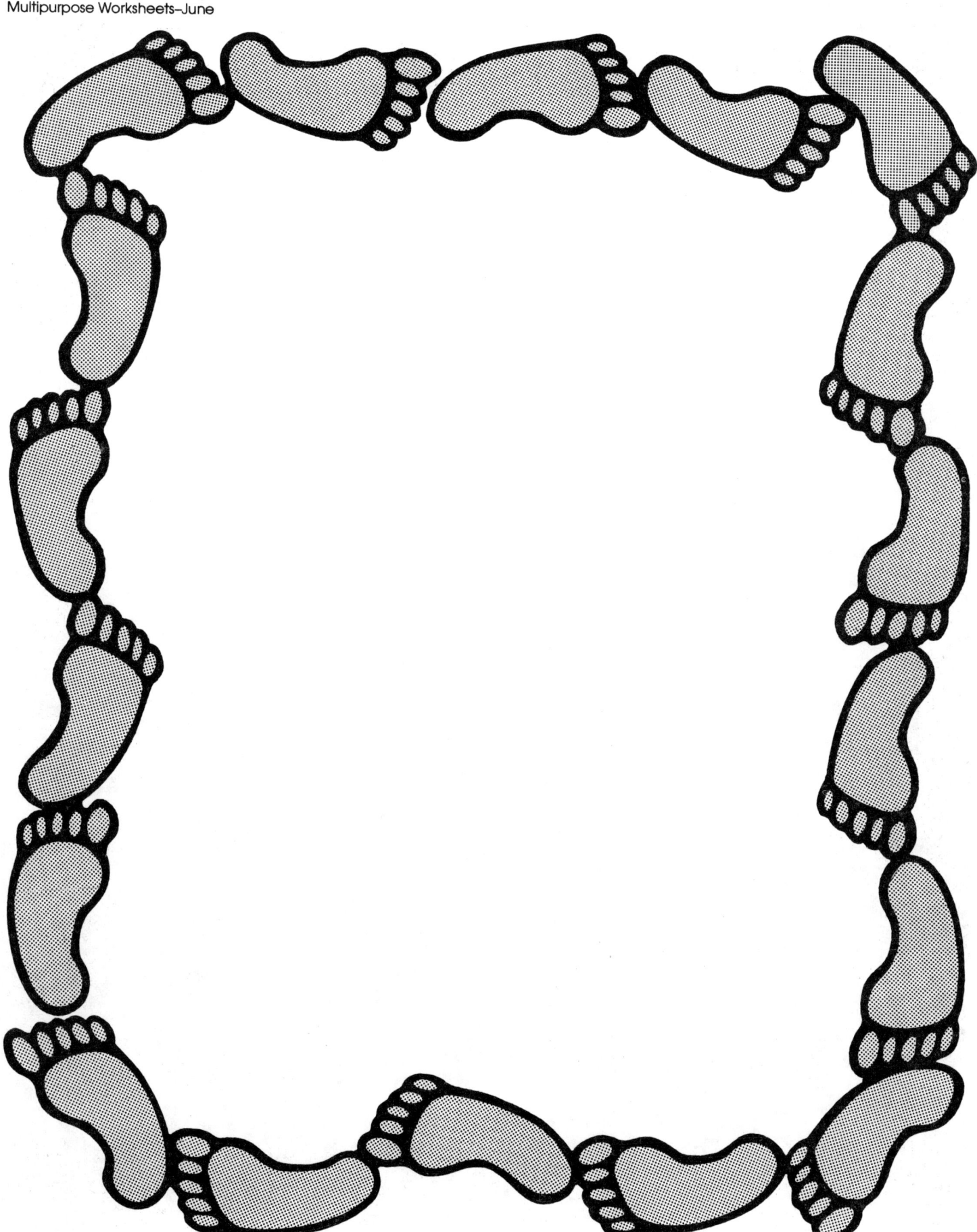

Art and Holiday Happenings
Clip Art

Clip Art

On pages 59-79 are theme-related drawings that you can use to create your own activity cards, announcements, awards, contracts, flyers, game boards, invitations, name tags, and programs, and to add a touch of whimsy to worksheets and tests. These drawings are grouped by subject or theme.

Although this art is theme-related, it is readily available to any classroom occasion or school year event. All you need to do is duplicate the page (so you can use the clip art on the other side later), cut out the drawing you wish to use, attach it to the sheet you intend to decorate, and reproduce the sheet with art in place.

With the help of an opaque projector or squared paper, you can enlarge clip art drawings for other applications. For example, you can make them large enough for effective use on bulletin boards, posters, and signs. You can also use them as patterns for book covers, borders, greeting cards, and other student- or teacher-made art.

Art and Holiday Happenings
Clip Art

Farm Animals

The Preschool Teacher's Pet
©1989–The Learning Works, Inc.

Art and Holiday Happenings
Clip Art

Wild Animals

Art and Holiday Happenings
Clip Art

Water Animals

Art and Holiday Happenings
Clip Art

Prehistoric Creatures

Art and Holiday Happenings
Clip Art

Things to Eat

The Preschool Teacher's Pet
©1989—The Learning Works, Inc.

Art and Holiday Happenings
Clip Art

More Things to Eat

Art and Holiday Happenings
Clip Art

Toys and Games

The Preschool Teacher's Pet
©1989–The Learning Works, Inc.

Art and Holiday Happenings
Clip Art

Holidays and Seasons – Winter

Art and Holiday Happenings
Clip Art

Holidays and Seasons – Spring and Summer

The Preschool Teacher's Pet
©1989–The Learning Works, Inc.

Community Helpers

Art and Holiday Happenings
Clip Art

Community Helpers
(continued)

Community Helpers
(continued)

Art and Holiday Happenings
Clip Art

Community Helpers
(continued)

mail carrier

janitor

construction worker

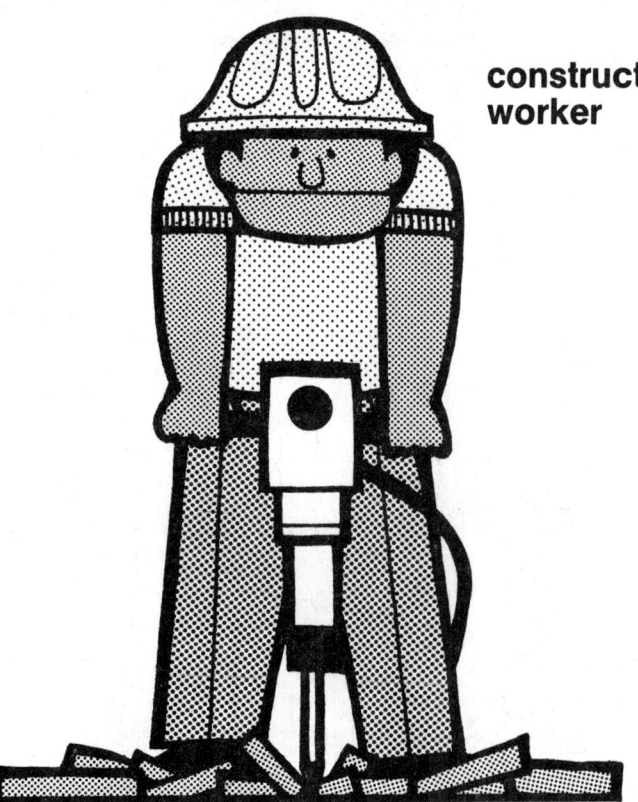

doctor

Art and Holiday Happenings
Clip Art

Community Helpers
(continued)

electrician

computer programmer

police officer

artist

The Preschool Teacher's Pet
©1989–The Learning Works, Inc.

Community Helpers
(continued)

Art and Holiday Happenings
Clip Art

Space Race

The Preschool Teacher's Pet
©1989–The Learning Works, Inc.

Borders

Borders cover rough edges, make any display look more finished, and add a seasonal or holiday touch to subject matter bulletin boards. They can easily be cut paper-doll style from folded lengths of paper or fabric.

Colored construction paper is probably the most widely used border material; however, for interesting effects, try felt, foil, gift wrap, newspaper, patterned shelf paper, plaid or print fabric, or wallpaper. For variety, combine and overlap borders of different but compatible shapes or borders of the same shape cut from paper or fabric of different shades or colors.

To create a border, first decide whether you intend to run bands across the top and bottom, down the sides, or entirely around your board. Measure this distance in inches. Divide the total distance in inches by the length of a single strip of paper or fabric, also in inches, to determine how many strips you need. Cut that number of strips.

Fold each strip in half and then in half again. Photocopy or trace any of the patterns on pages 81-90. Position the pattern on your folded paper or fabric as shown, draw around it with a pencil or chalk, and cut out the resulting shape. Carefully unfold the strip.

The borders on the following pages have been designed to make efficient use of a 12-inch-by-18-inch piece of construction paper. Most of them can be cut from either a folded 12-inch strip or a folded 18-inch strip. Note the dimensions given beside each pattern.

Art and Holiday Happenings
Borders—September

Squirrels and Leaves

Squirrels

Let these frisky critters scamper across the board to welcome your students to school. Cut squirrels from 3½-inch-by-18-inch strips folded to be 3½-inch-by-4½-inch rectangles. Use a felt pen or crayon to add eyes and smiles.

Oak Leaves

Cut from 4-inch-by-18-inch strips folded to be 4-inch-by-4½-inch rectangles. For best results, place the stem edge on the thick fold. Vary by using red, orange, yellow, and brown paper and mixing or overlapping strips of different colors. For spring, use shades of green.

Art and Holiday Happenings
Borders–October

Pumpkins and Ghosts

Pumpkins

Cut from 4-inch-by-18-inch strips folded to be 4-inch-by-4½-inch rectangles. For variety, separately cut brown or green stems and glue them over the existing ones. Just for fun, use a black felt-tipped marking pen to transform some or all of the pumpkins into jack-o'-lanterns. Follow the pattern suggested here or create your own.

Ghosts

Make a row of grinning ghosts to dance across your bulletin board. Cut them from 4-inch-by-18-inch strips folded to be 4-inch-by-4½-inch rectangles.

thick fold

Turkeys and Corn

Turkeys

Thanksgiving wouldn't be complete without a turkey. Here's a whole flock of them to band or border your bulletin boards. Cut them from 4-inch-by-12-inch strips folded to be 4-inch-by-3-inch rectangles.

thick fold

Corn

Celebrate Thanksgiving's harvest with ears of corn. Cut from 3-inch-by-18-inch strips of green or brown paper folded to be 3-inch-by-4½-inch rectangles. Separately cut the ear shapes from yellow paper and glue them in place.

Bells and Bows

Bells

Bells ring out the old year and ring in the new. Cut them from 4-inch-by-12-inch strips folded to be 4-inch-by-3-inch rectangles. Add colored stripes or other decorations if desired.

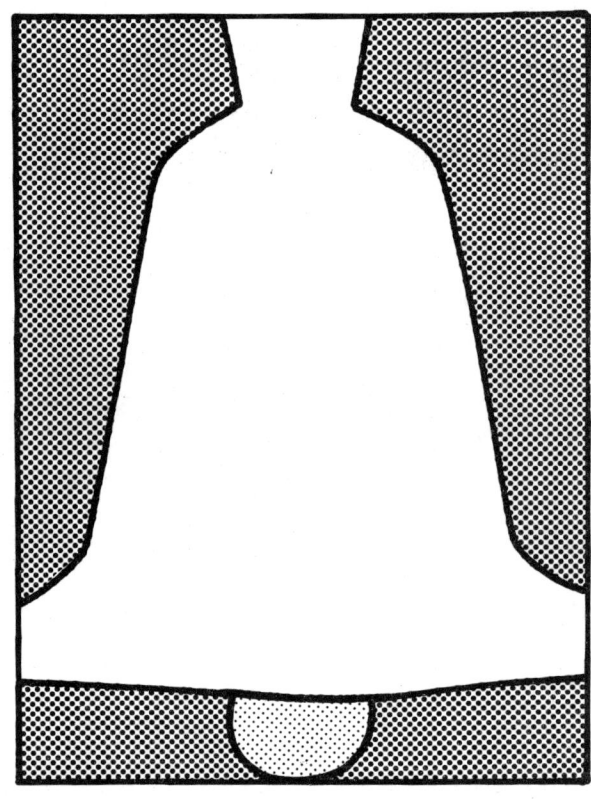

Bows

Make these festive bows out of any colorful paper. Cut them from 4-inch-by-18-inch strips folded to be 4-inch-by-4½-inch rectangles.

Snowmen and Hats

Snowmen

Welcome winter with a row of men made of snow. Cut them from 4½-inch-by-12-inch strips folded to be 4½-inch-by-3-inch rectangles. Just for fun, use a black felt-tipped marking pen to give some or all of your snowmen a black top hat, black eyes, a button nose, and a friendly smile.

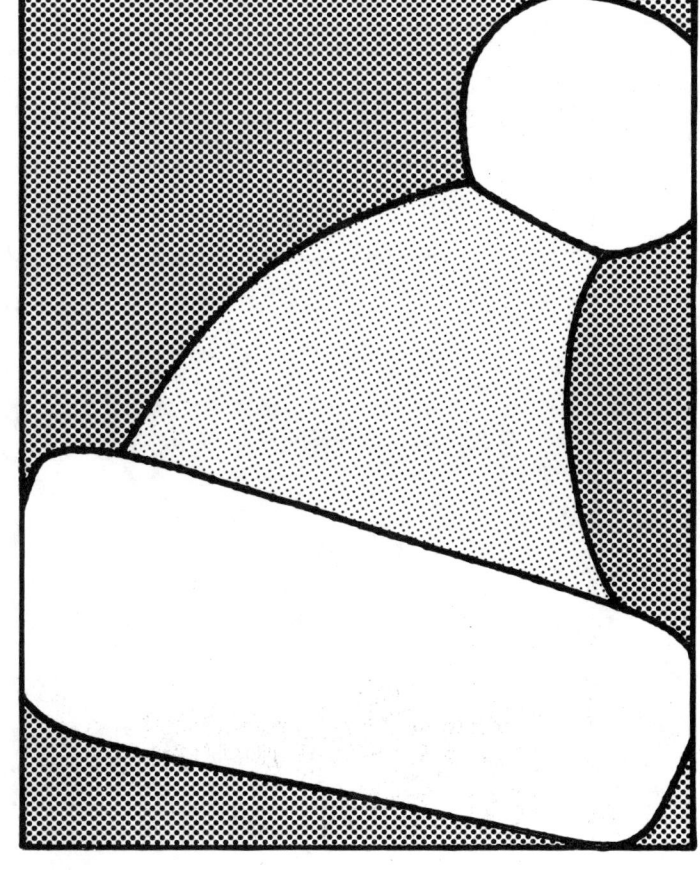

Winter Hats

Keep cozy in the cold with these colorful hats. Cut them from 4½-inch-by-14-inch strips folded to be 4½-inch-by-3½-inch rectangles. Use crayons or felt pens to color the area which is lightly shaded in the pattern.

Hatchets and Hearts

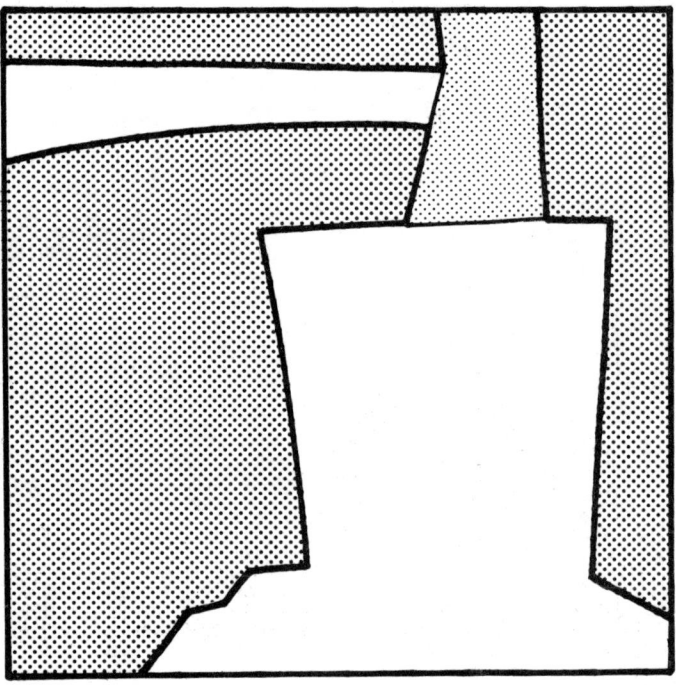

Hatchets

Lincoln the log-splitter often used a handy hatchet. Cut these from 3½-inch-by-14-inch strips folded to be 3½-inch-by-3½-inch squares. Use a silver crayon, paint, or foil to color the hatchet blades.

Hearts

Greet February with a row of Valentine hearts. Cut them from 4-inch-by-18-inch strips of red paper folded to be 4-inch-by-4½-inch rectangles. Round the corners, then fold the rectangles in half again to cut out the heart shapes. You may wish to glue 3-inch-by-4-inch pieces of pink paper behind the heart-shaped holes.

Shamrocks and Tulips

Shamrocks

Sure an' begorra, St. Patrick's Day is the time to wish for the luck o' the Irish and to wear a little green. Cut these shamrocks from 4-inch-by-18-inch strips folded to be 4-inch-by-4½-inch rectangles.

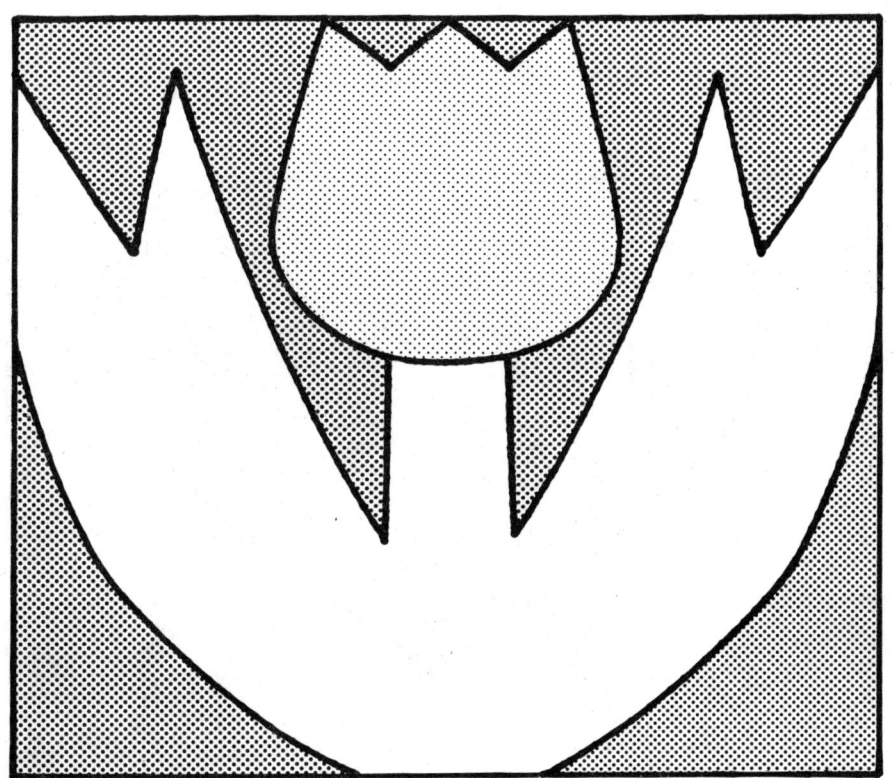

Tulips

Welcome spring with these familiar flowers. Cut them from 4-inch-by-18-inch strips folded to be 4-inch-by-4½-inch rectangles. If desired, use green for the basic border shape and add flowers cut from paper in assorted bright colors.

Ducks and Bunnies

Ducks

These happy ducks love April's showers. Cut them from 4-inch-by-16-inch strips folded to be 4-inch-by-4-inch squares. Use felt pens to add eyes and color the beaks and feet.

Bunches of Bunnies

For Easter or for spring, border a bulletin board with a bunch of bunnies. Cut them from 4½-inch-by-12-inch strips folded to be 4½-inch-by-3-inch rectangles. For variety, cut bunnies from paper in pastel colors rather than from white. Just for fun, use a felt-tipped marking pen to draw facial features on some or all of your bunnies. Follow the pattern provided here or create your own.

Daisies and Suns

Daisies

April showers bring May flowers. Freshen your room with dozens of daisies. Cut them from 4-inch-by-8-inch white strips folded to be 4-inch-by-2-inch rectangles. For best results, place the daisy center on the thick fold. After cutting, carefully unfold each two-daisy strip. As a variation, use a crayon or felt-tipped marking pen to add yellow centers or cut them from yellow construction paper and glue them in place.

Suns

When May comes, the hot summer sun is not many days away. Cut these suns from yellow or orange 4-inch-by-16-inch-strips folded to be 4-inch-by-4-inch squares. As a variation, add 2¼-inch circles cut from a contrasting color of paper.

Art and Holiday Happenings
Borders–General

Dancers and Hands

Dancers

Snip out rows of happy children to dance across the wall. Cut them from 4-inch-by-18-inch strips folded to be 4-inch-by-4½-inch rectangles.

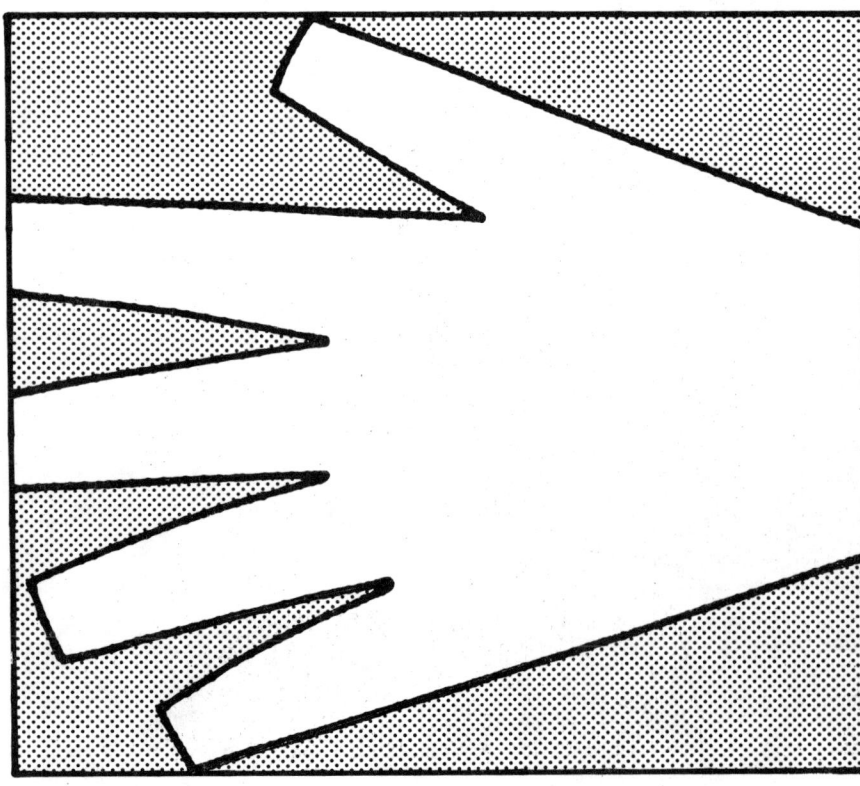

Hands

Let these helpful hands encircle a display of drawings or other projects. Cut the hands from 4-inch-by-18-inch strips folded to be 4-inch-by-4½-inch rectangles.

The Preschool Teacher's Pet
©1989–The Learning Works, Inc.

Numbers & Counting

Numbers and Counting
Numbers 1–10

Name _____

one

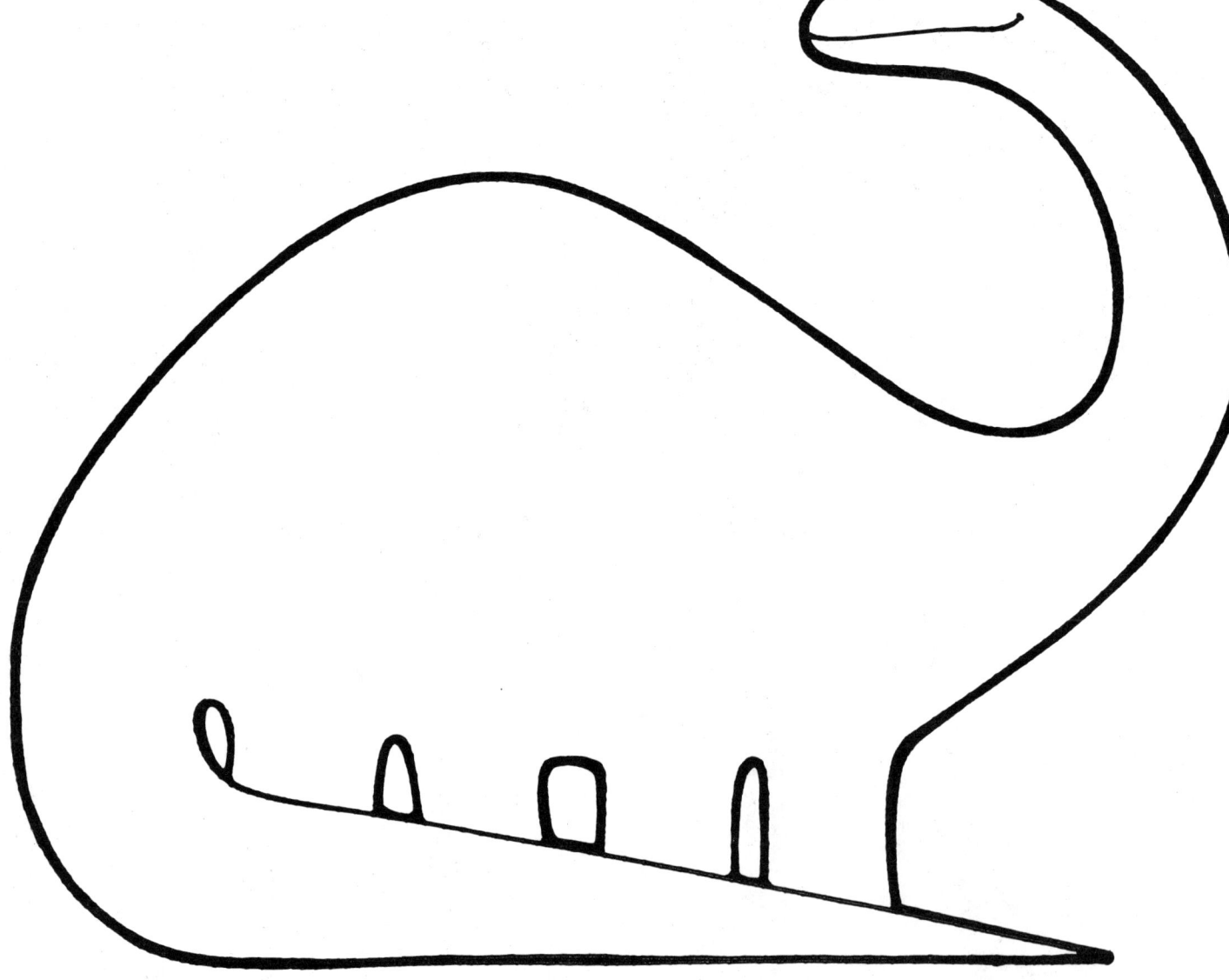

Numbers and Counting
Numbers 1–10

Name _____

two

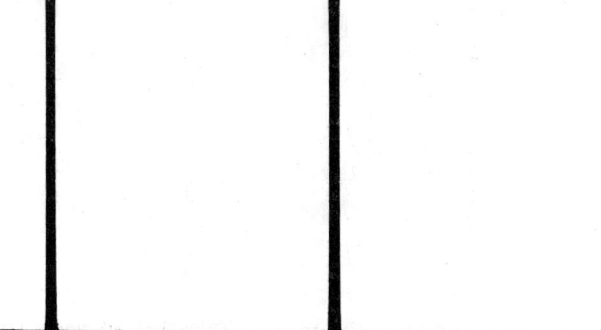

Numbers and Counting
Numbers 1–10

Name _____

three

Numbers and Counting
Numbers 1–10

Name _____

four

Numbers and Counting
Numbers 1–10

Name _____

five

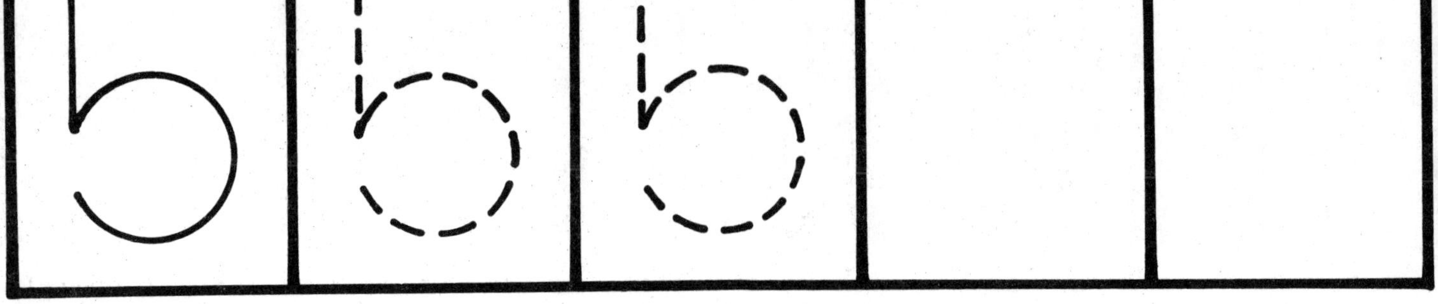

Numbers and Counting
Numbers 1–10

Name _____

six

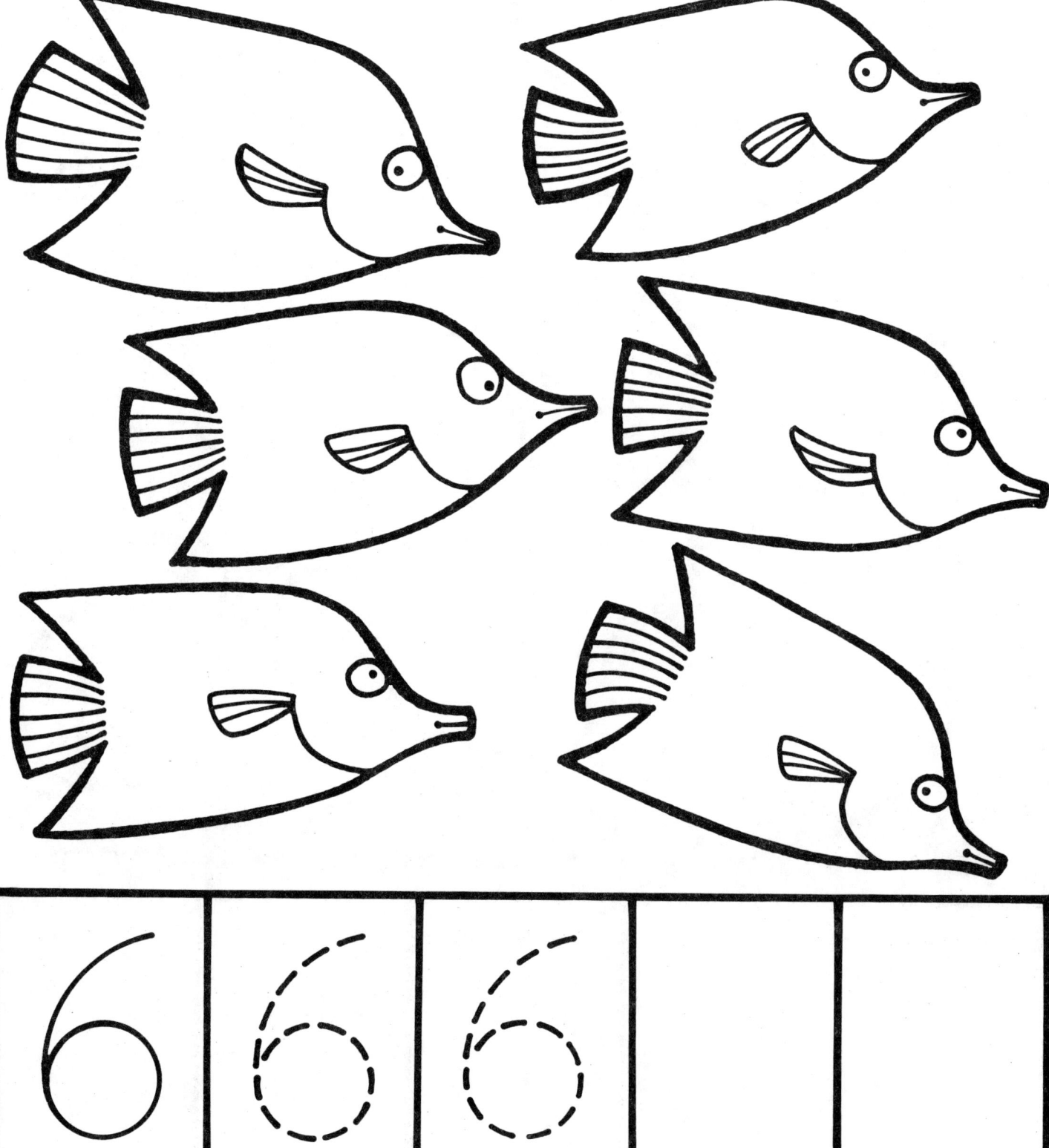

The Preschool Teacher's Pet
©1989–The Learning Works, Inc.

Numbers and Counting
Numbers 1–10

Name _____

seven

The Preschool Teacher's Pet
©1989–The Learning Works, Inc.
98

Numbers and Counting
Numbers 1–10

Name _____

eight

  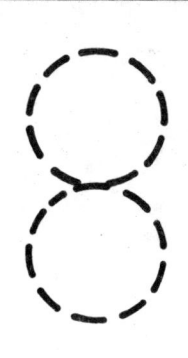

Numbers and Counting
Numbers 1–10

Name _____

nine

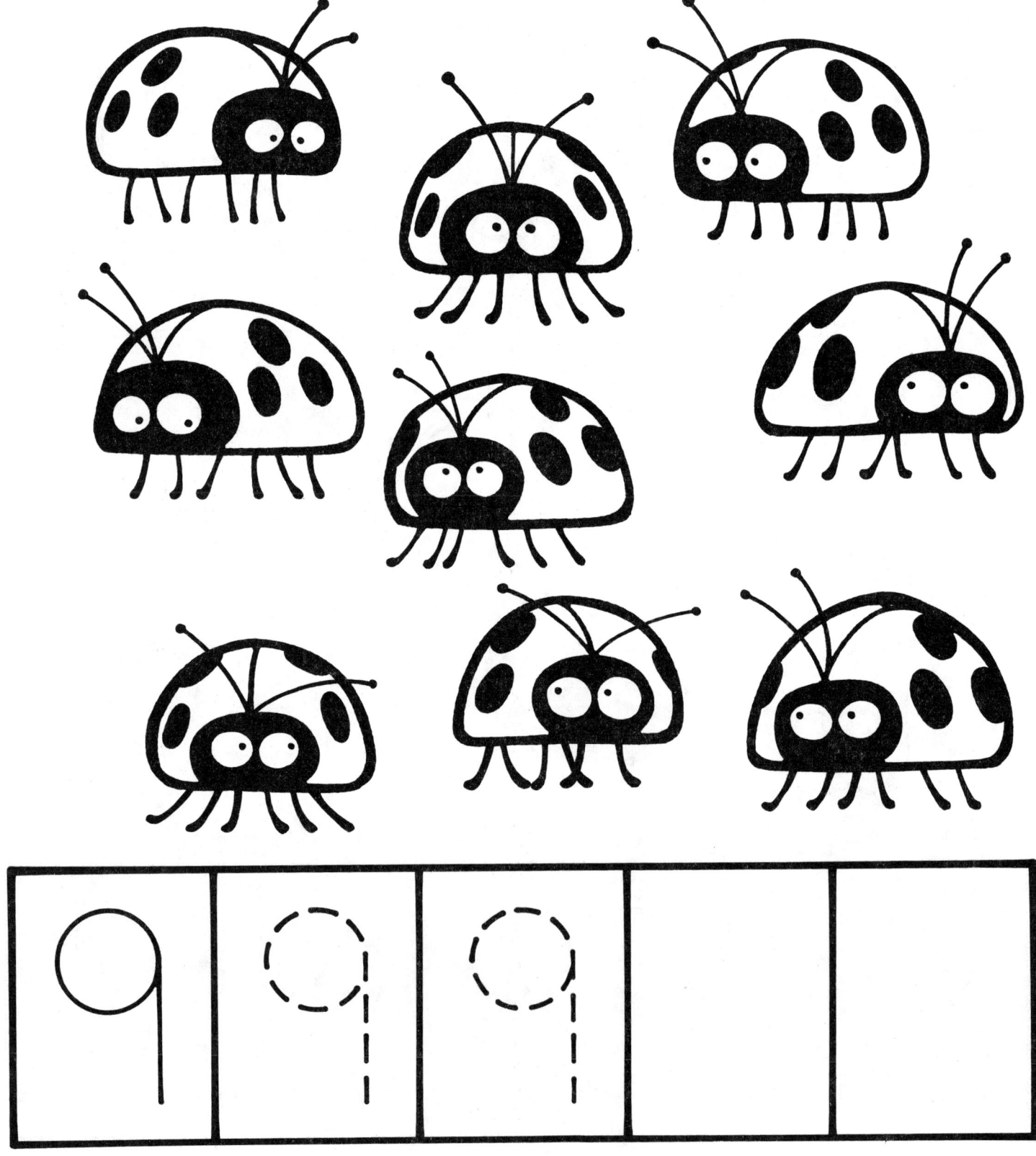

Numbers and Counting
Numbers 1–10

Name _____

ten

Numbers and Counting
Counting 1–10

Name _____

Circle the correct number.

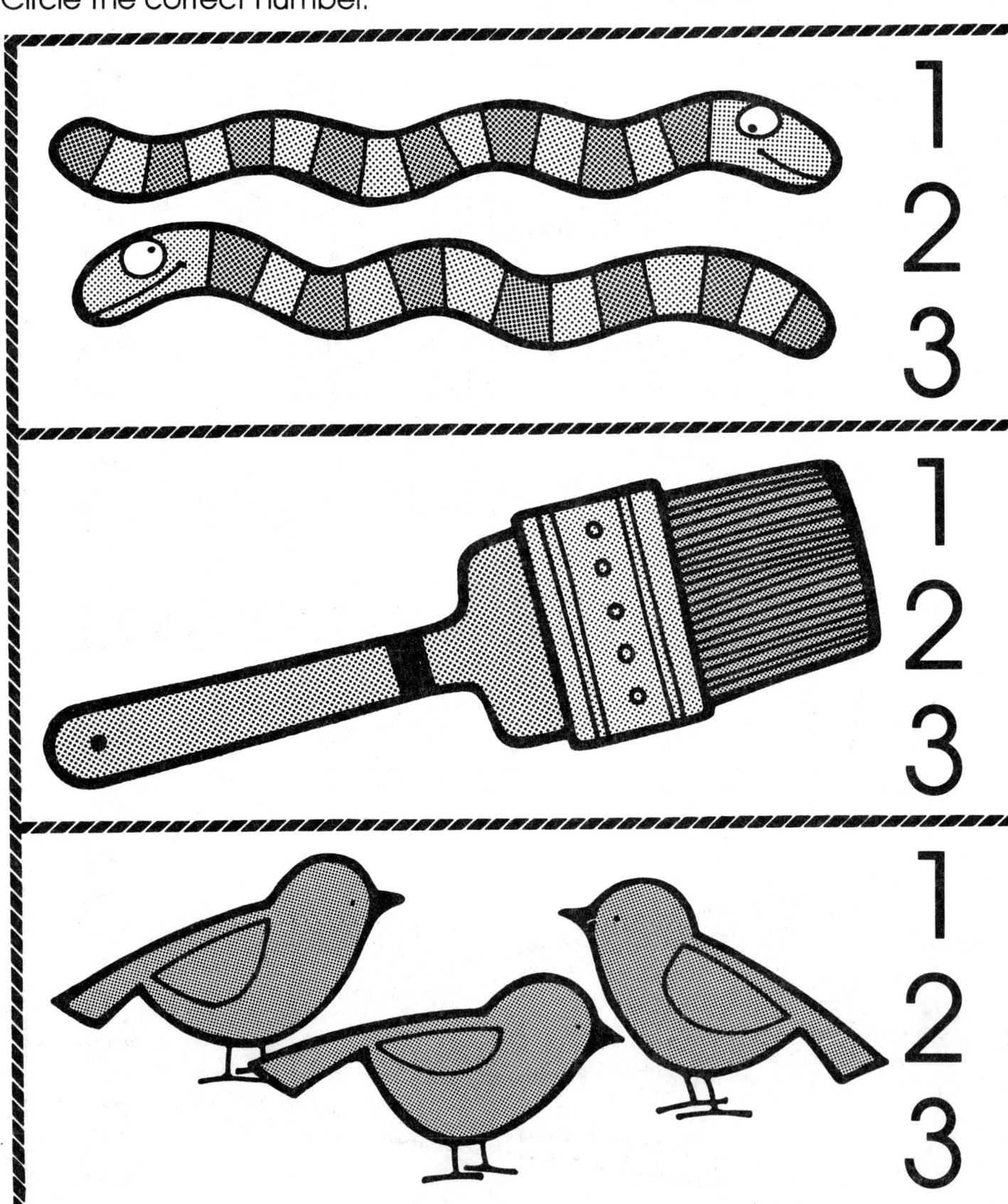

Numbers and Counting
Counting 1–10

Name _____

Circle the correct number.

Numbers and Counting
Counting 1–10

Name _____

Circle the correct number.

Numbers and Counting
Counting 1–10

Name _____

Circle the correct number.

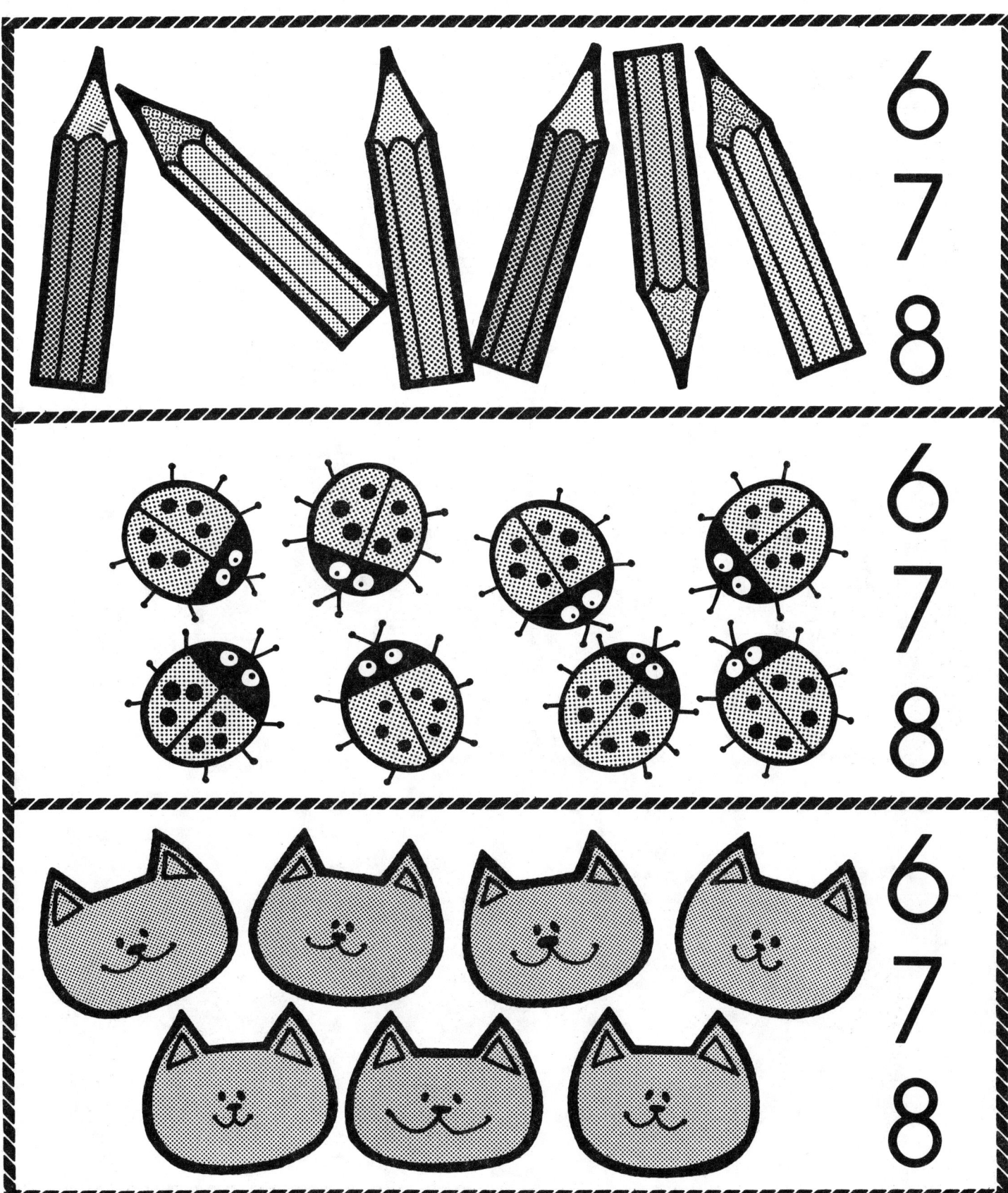

Numbers and COUNTING
Counting 1–10

Name _____

Circle the correct number.

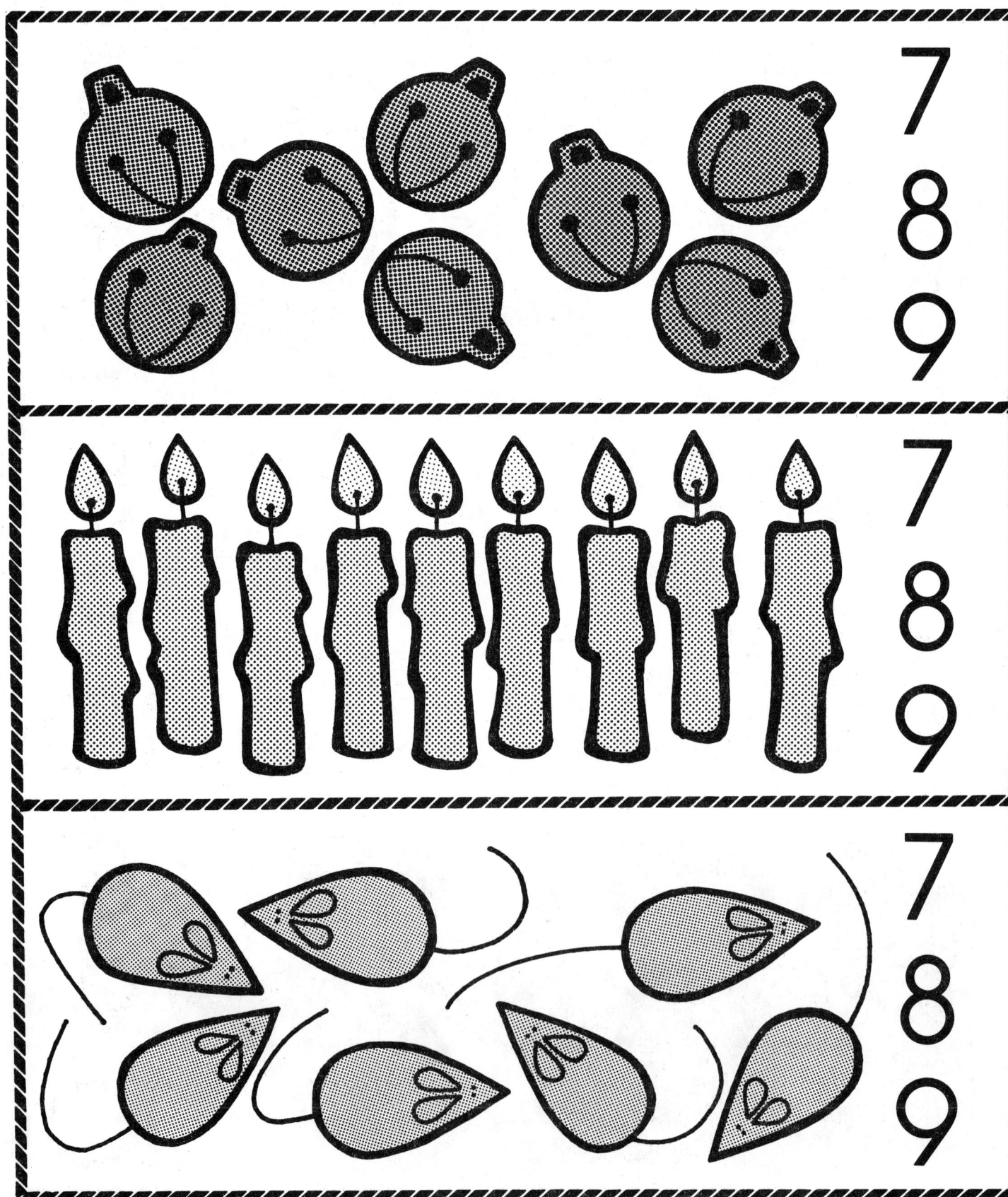

Numbers and Counting
Counting 1–10

Name _____

Circle the correct number.

Numbers and Counting
Counting 1–10

Name _____

Count the Candles

Count the candles. Paste the correct number in each square.

Numbers and Counting
Counting 1–10

Name _____

Count the Stars

Count the stars. Paste the correct number in each square.

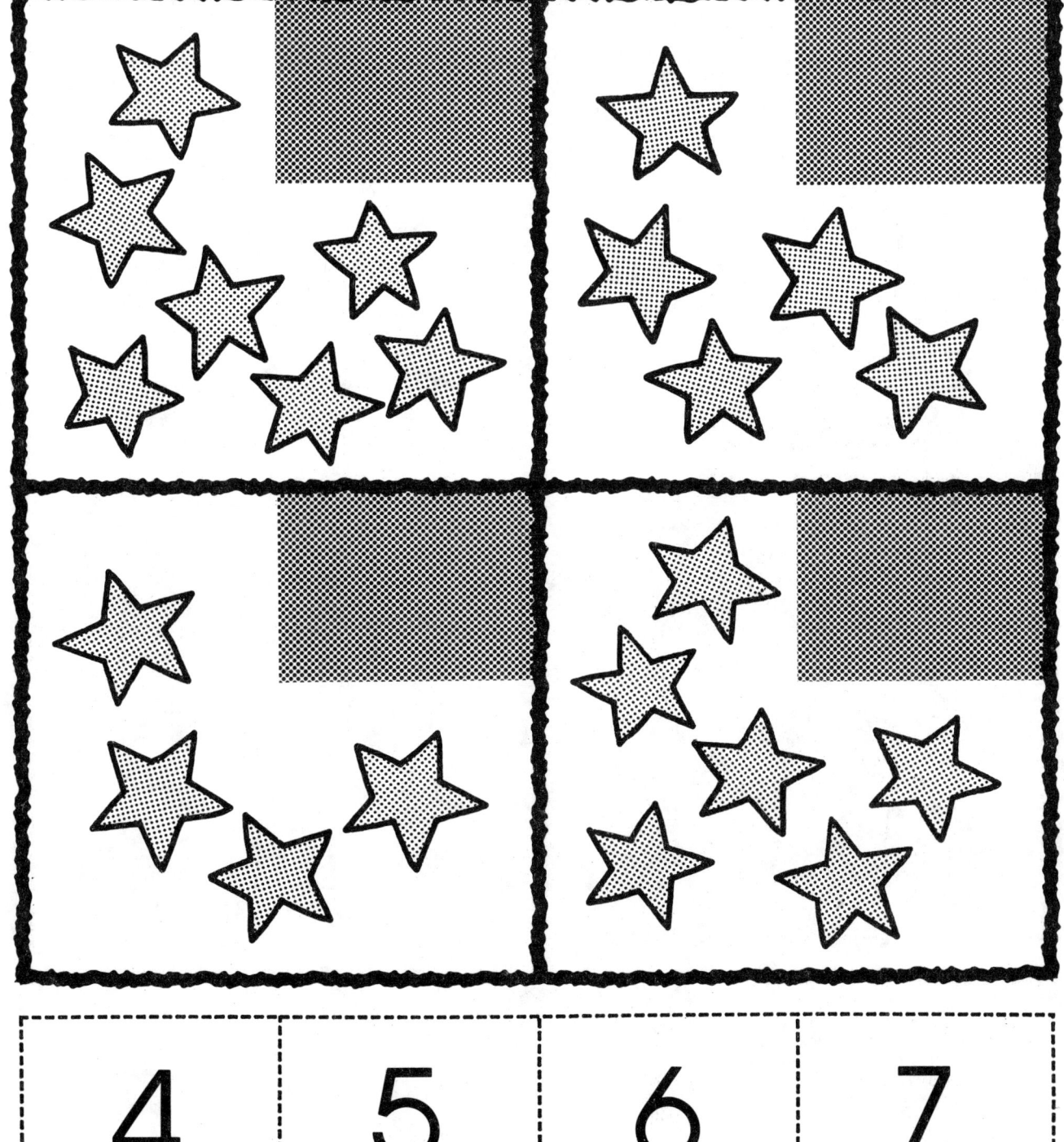

The Preschool Teacher's Pet
©1989–The Learning Works, Inc.

Numbers and Counting
Counting 1–10

Name _____

Count the Turtles

Count the turtles. Paste the correct number in each square.

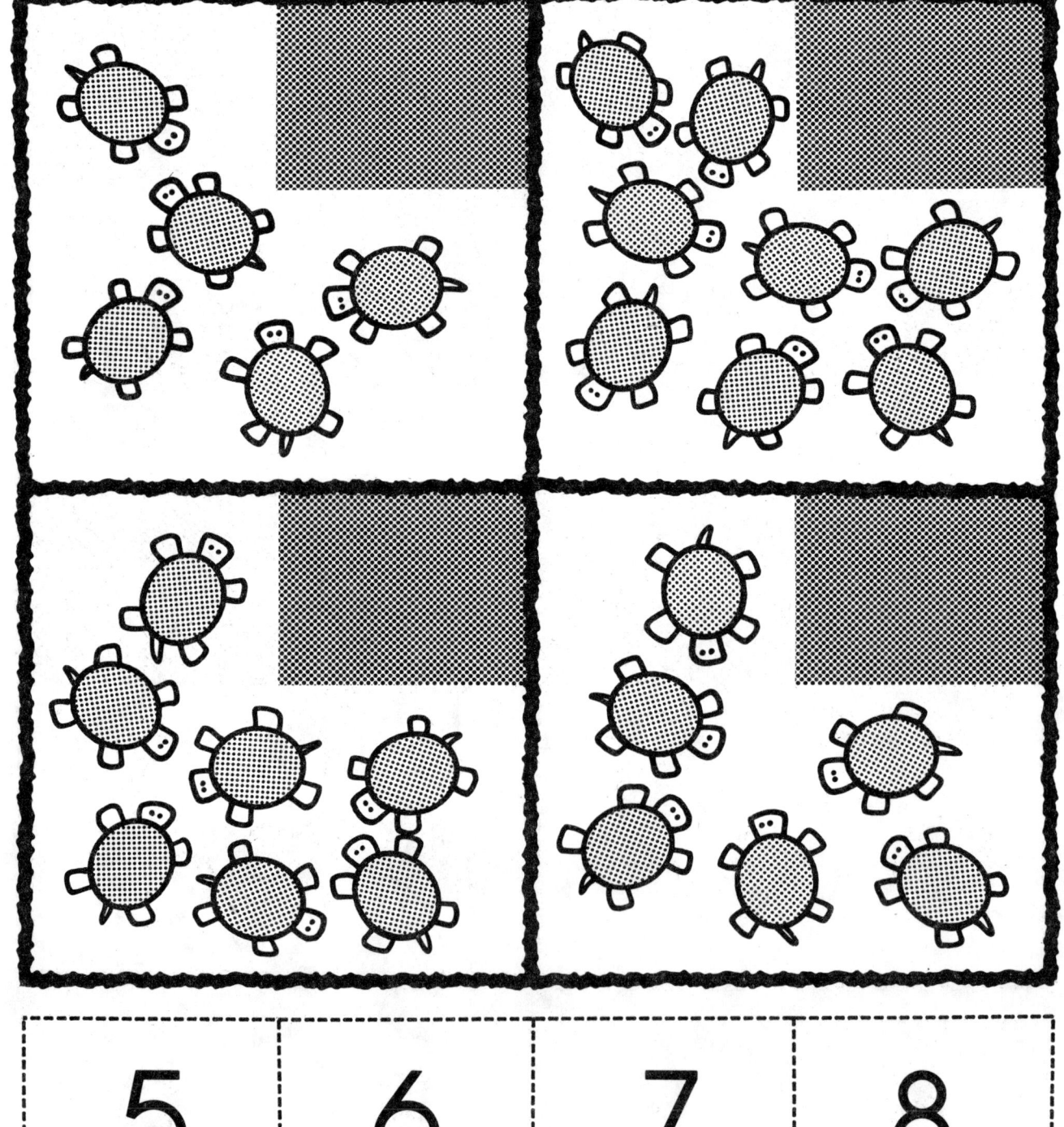

Numbers and Counting
Counting 1–10

Name _____

Count the Hearts

Count the hearts. Paste the correct number in each square.

The Preschool Teacher's Pet
©1989–The Learning Works, Inc.

Numbers and Counting
Counting 1-10

Name _____

Count the Rocks

Count the rocks. Paste the correct number in each square.

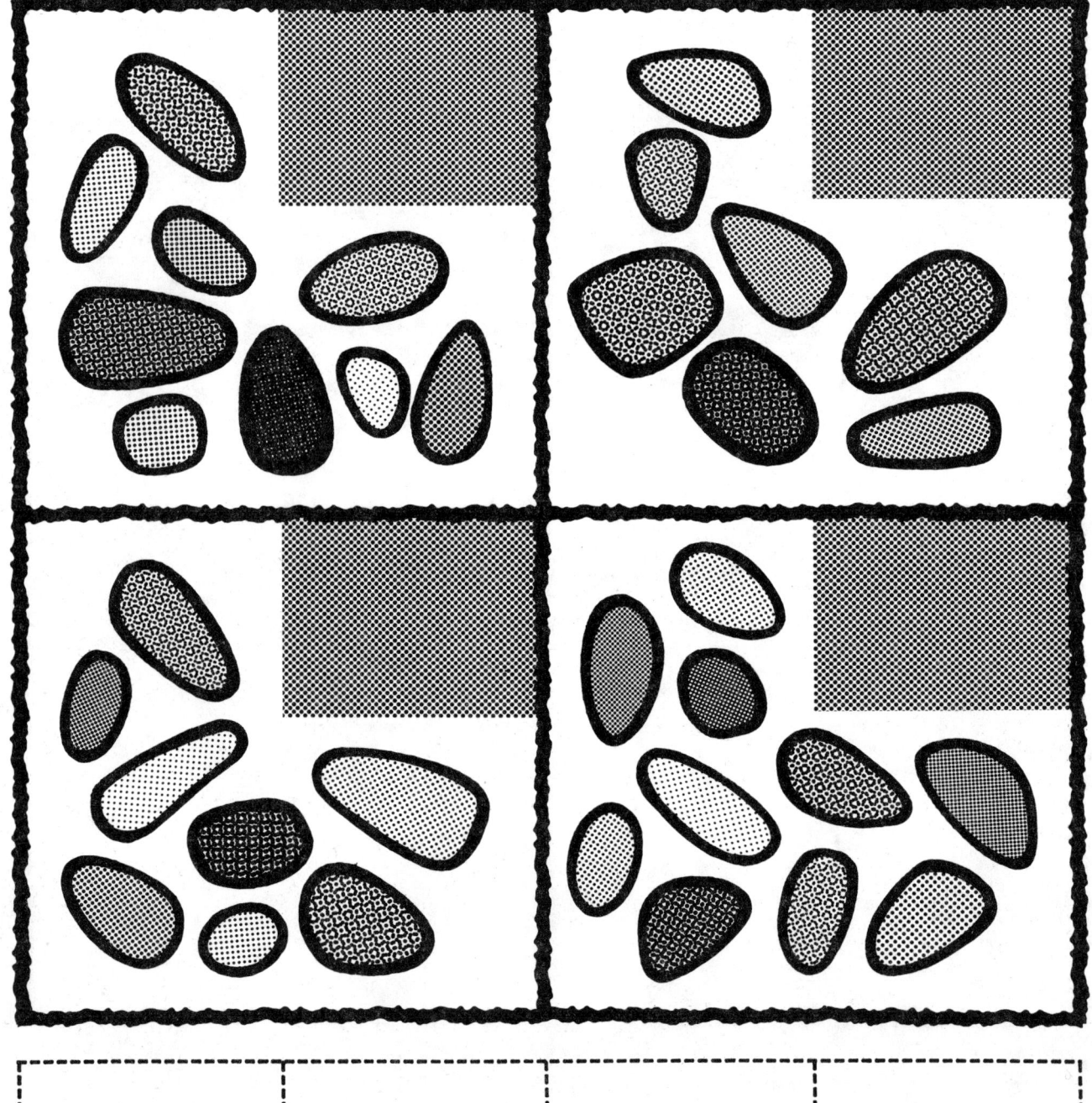

The Preschool Teacher's Pet
©1989–The Learning Works, Inc.

The Alphabet
Letters of the Alphabet

Name _____

alligator

A A   a a

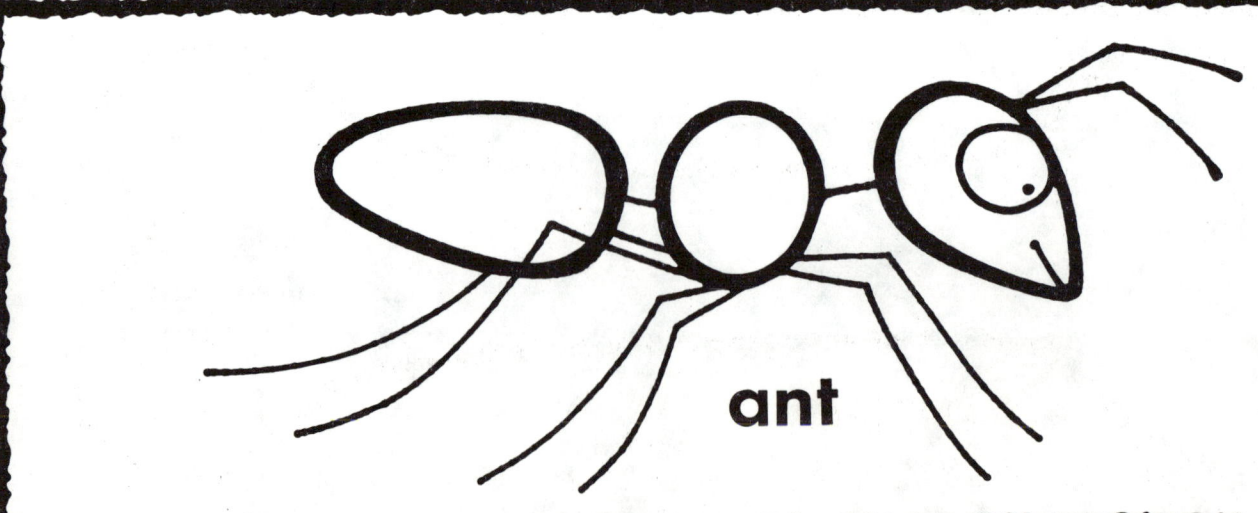

ant

The Alphabet
Letters of the Alphabet

Name _____

butterfly

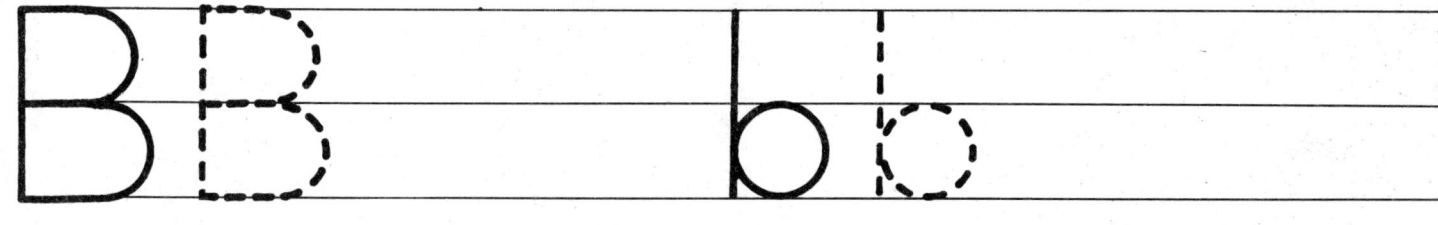

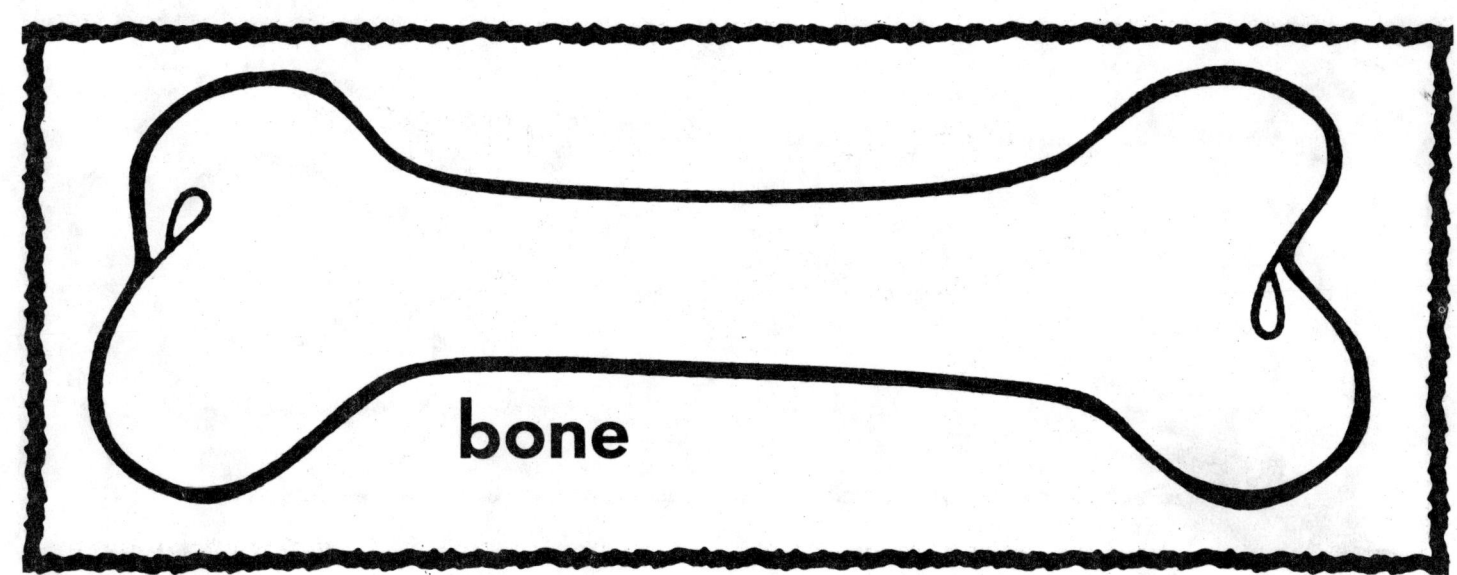

bone

The Alphabet
Letters of the Alphabet

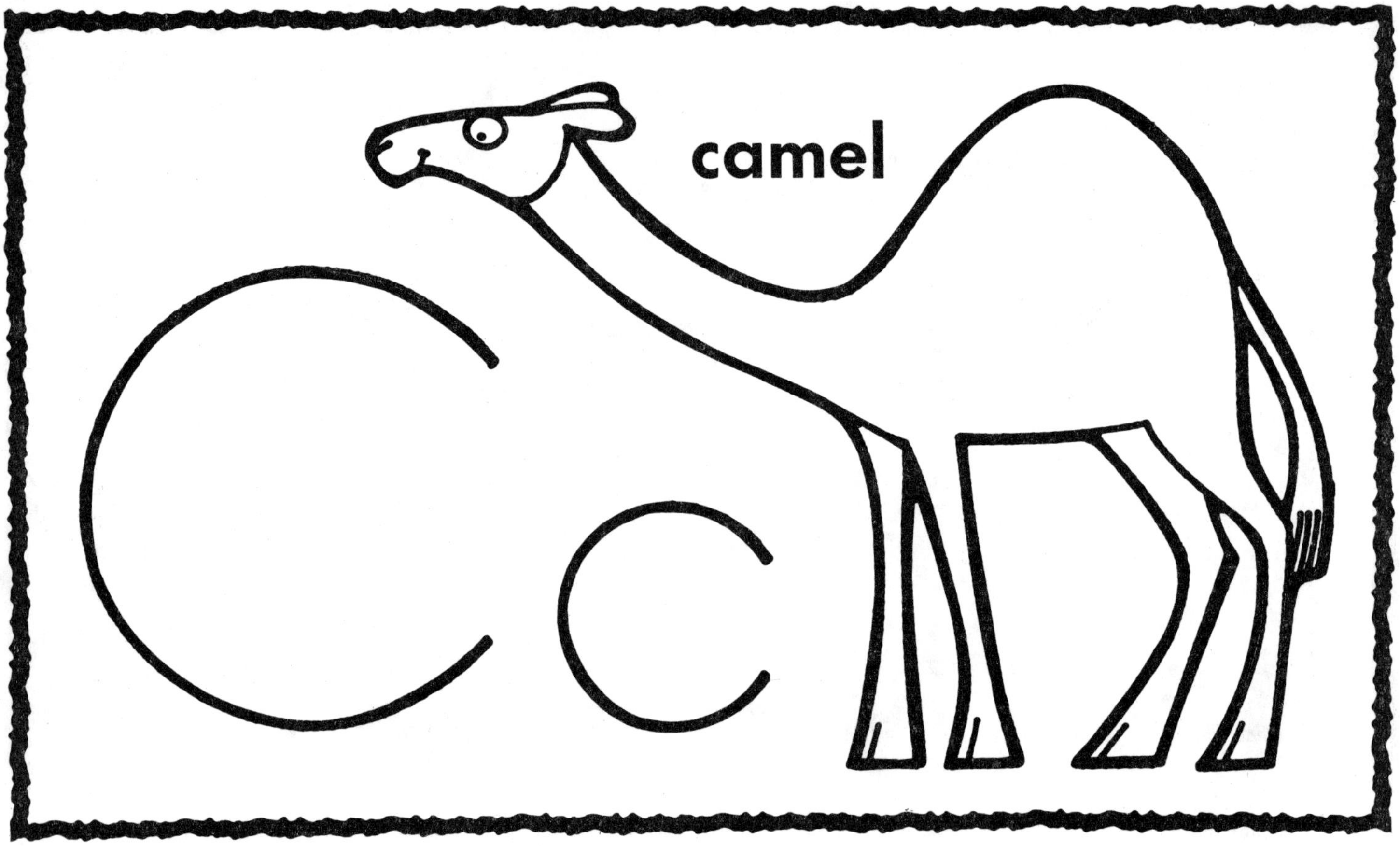

Name _____

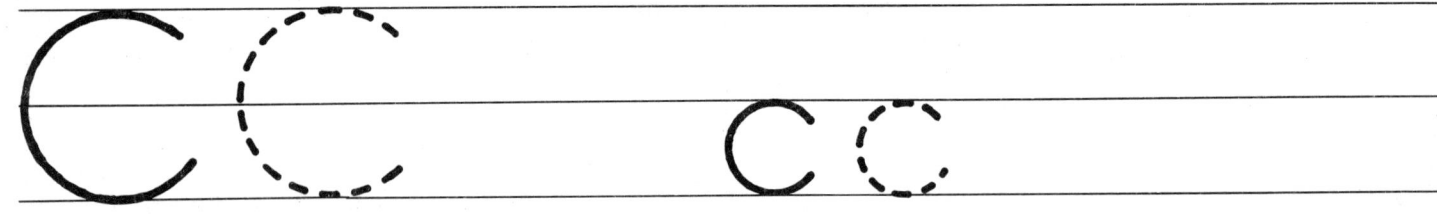

The Alphabet
Letters of the Alphabet

Name _____

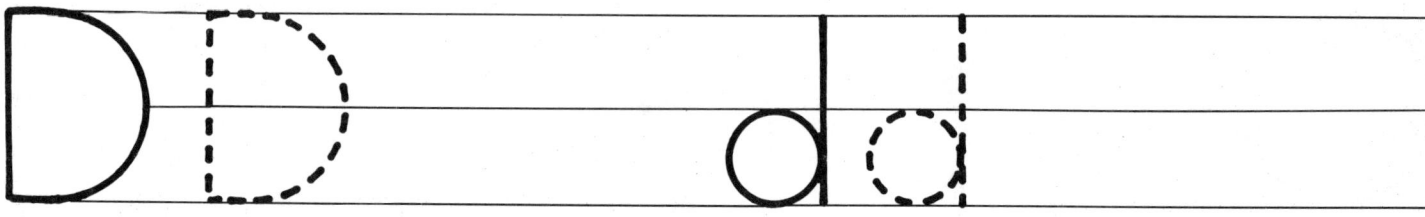

duck

dog

The Alphabet
Letters of the Alphabet

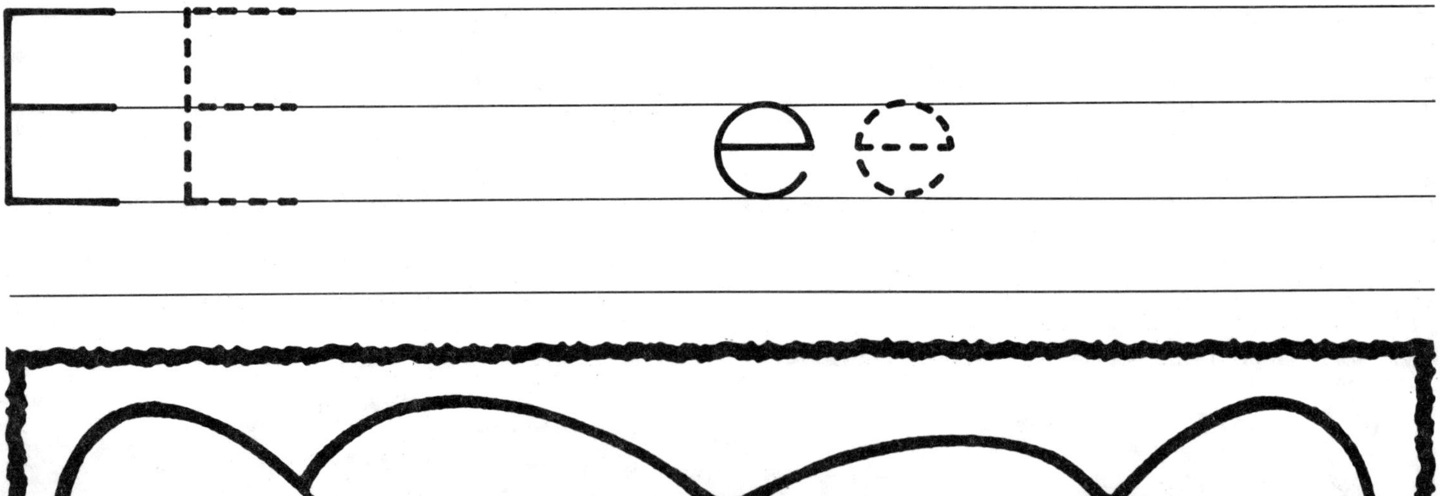

Name _____

elephant

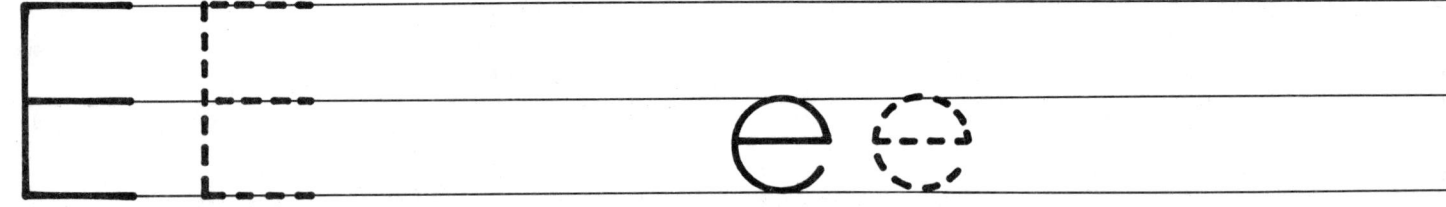

eggs

The Alphabet
Letters of the Alphabet

Name _____

F f

fish

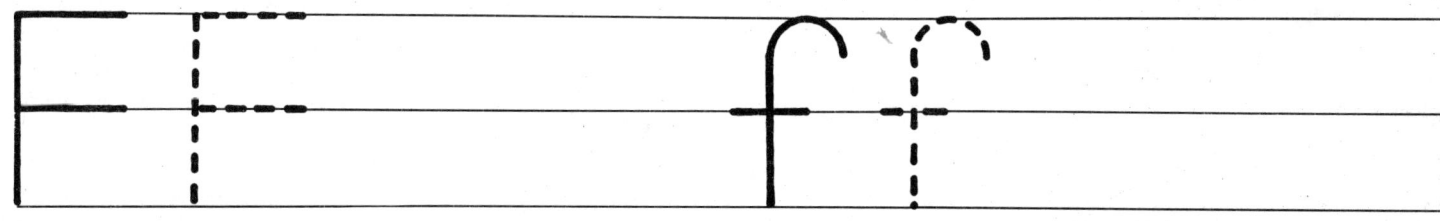

frog

The Alphabet
Letters of the Alphabet

Name _____

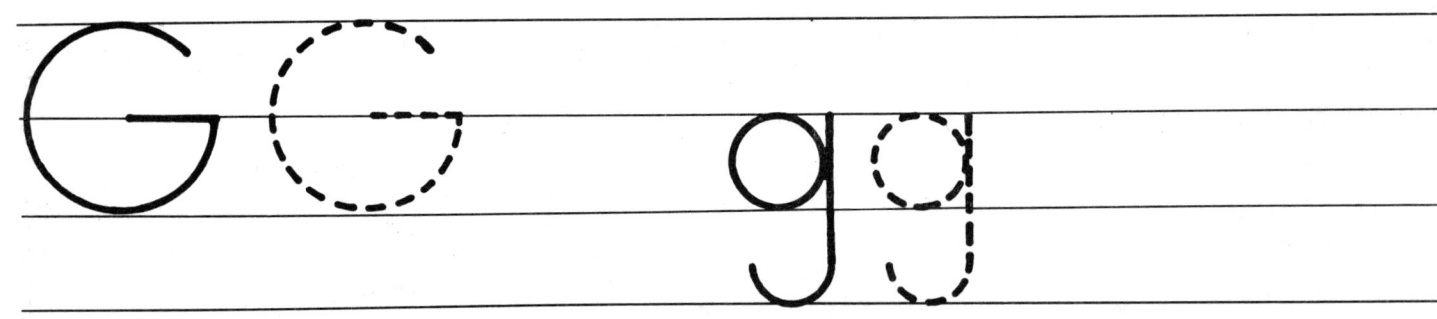

giraffe

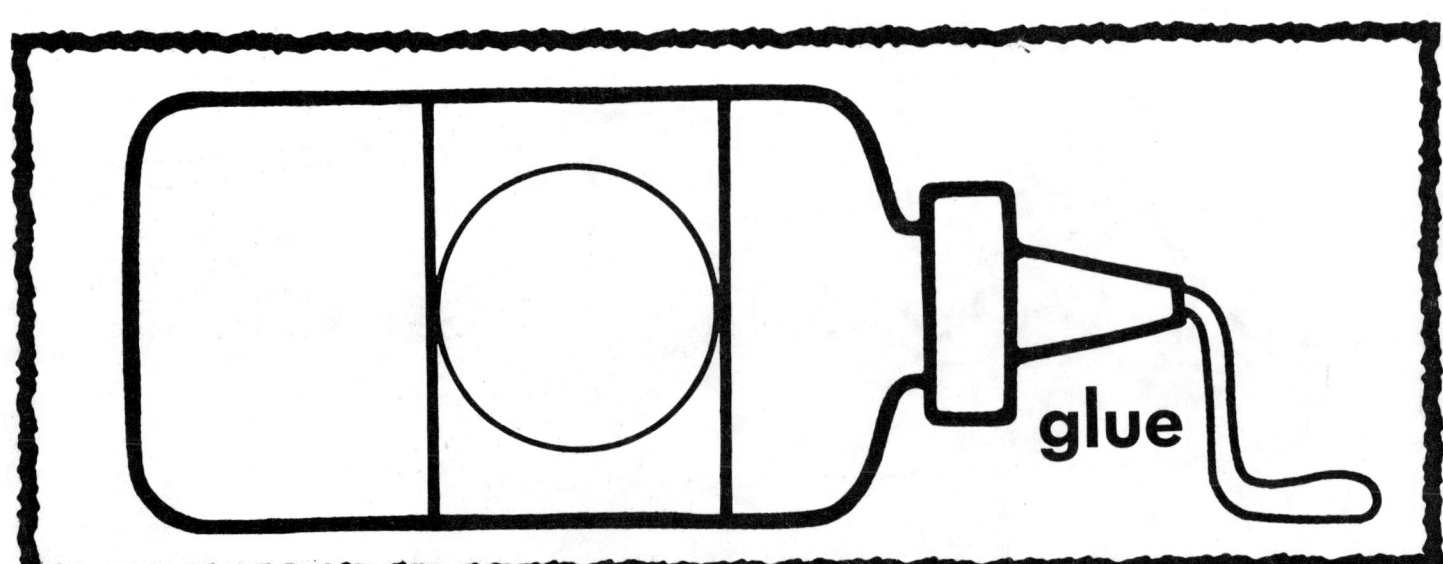

glue

The Alphabet
Letters of the Alphabet

Name _____

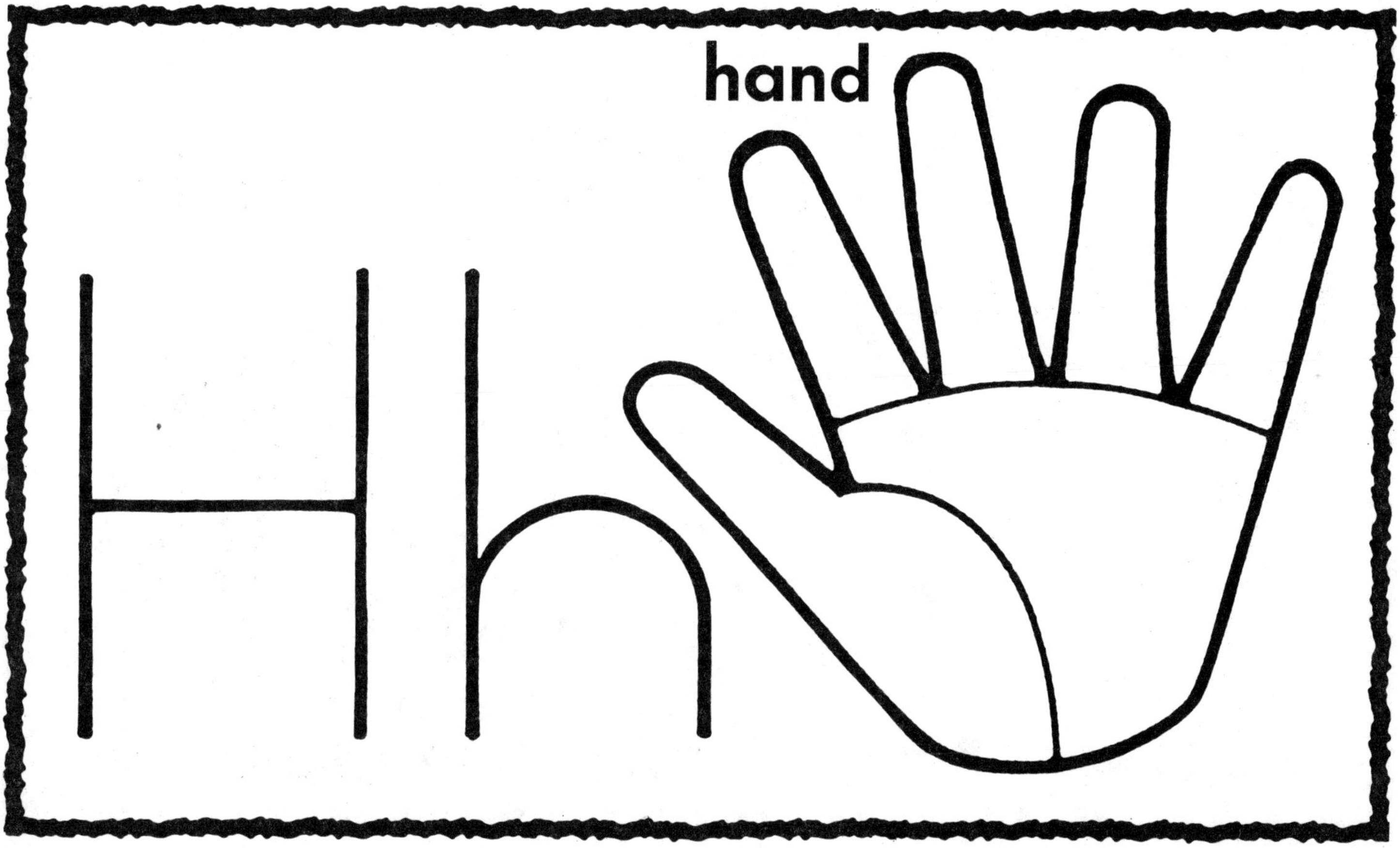

Hh   hand

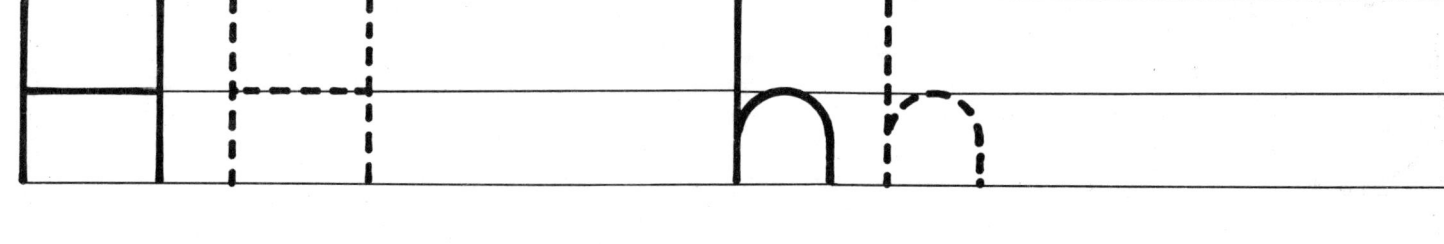

helicopter

The Preschool Teacher's Pet
©1989—The Learning Works, Inc.

The Alphabet
Letters of the Alphabet

Name _____

igloo

I i

island

The Preschool Teacher's Pet
©1989–The Learning Works, Inc.

122

The Alphabet
Letters of the Alphabet

Name _____

Jj

jam

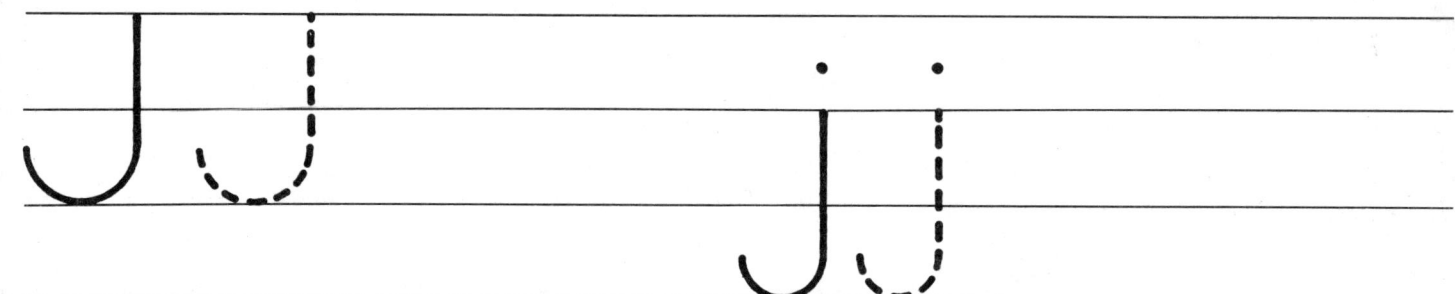

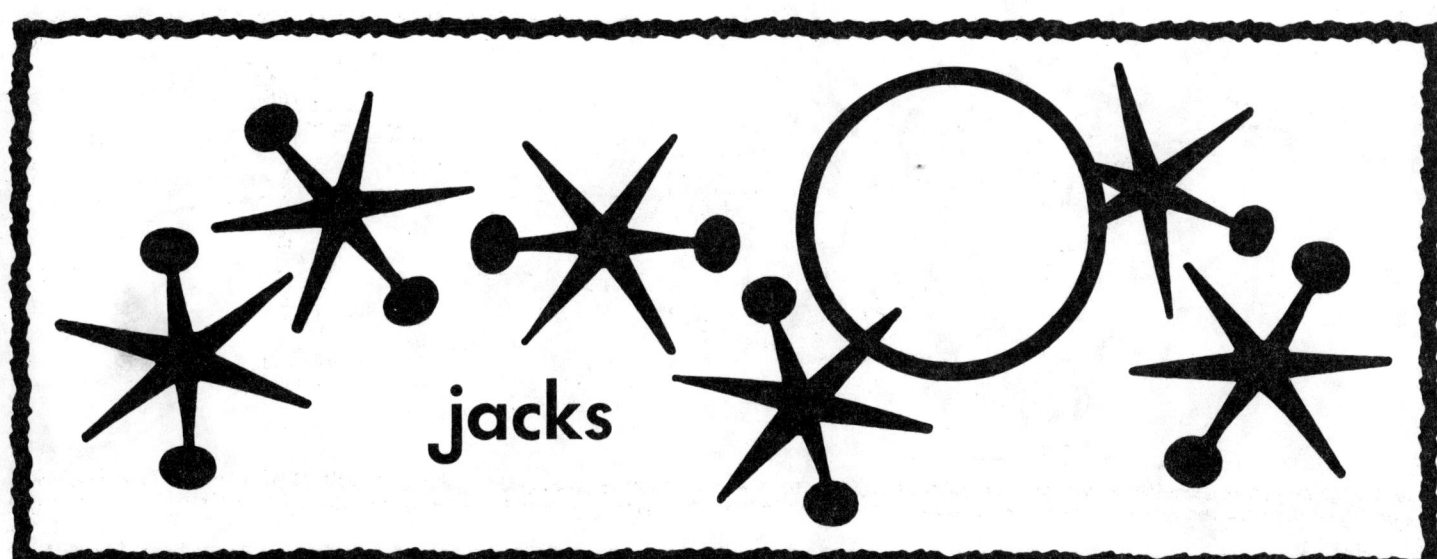

jacks

The Preschool Teacher's Pet
©1989–The Learning Works, Inc.

The Alphabet
Letters of the Alphabet

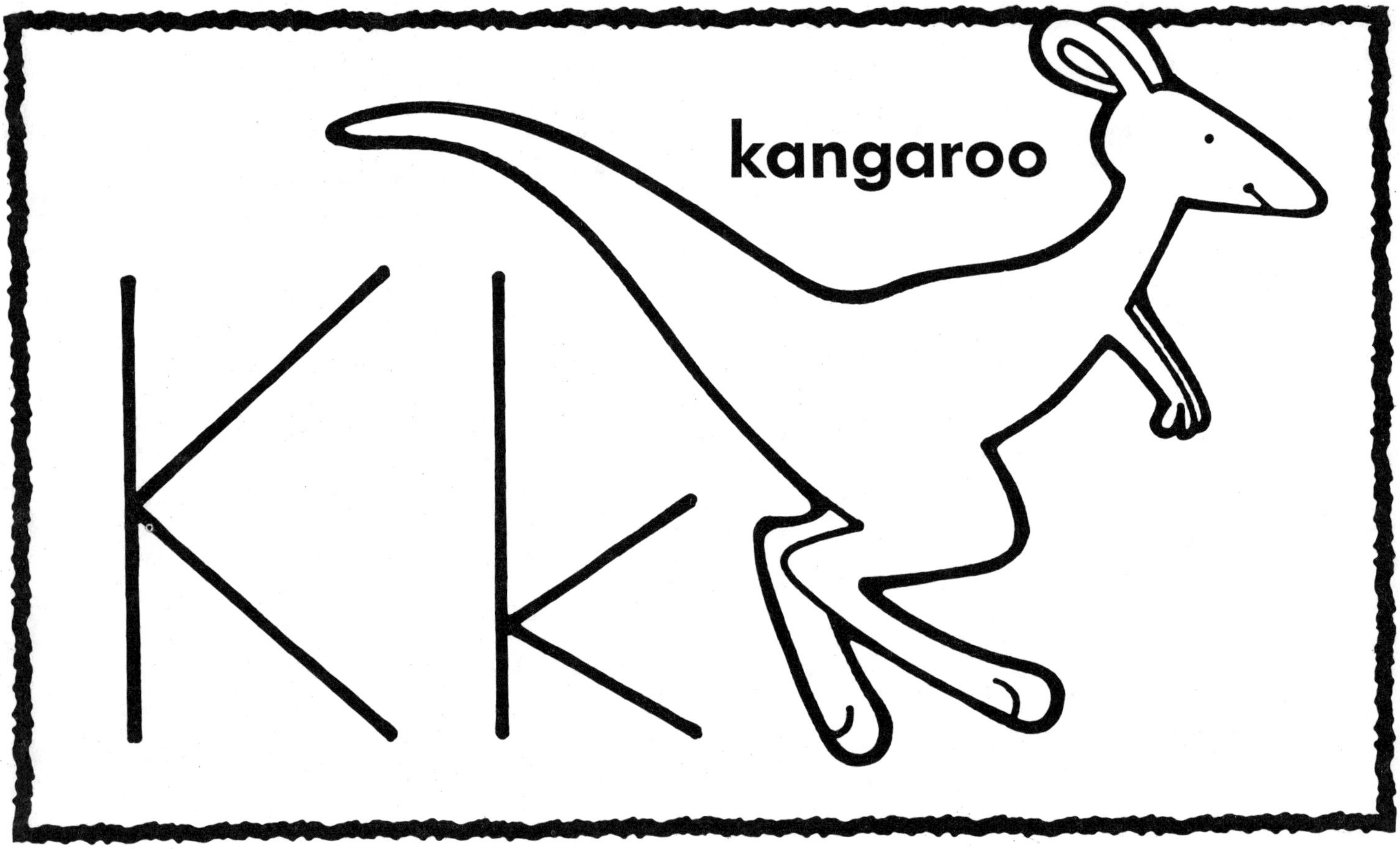

Name _____

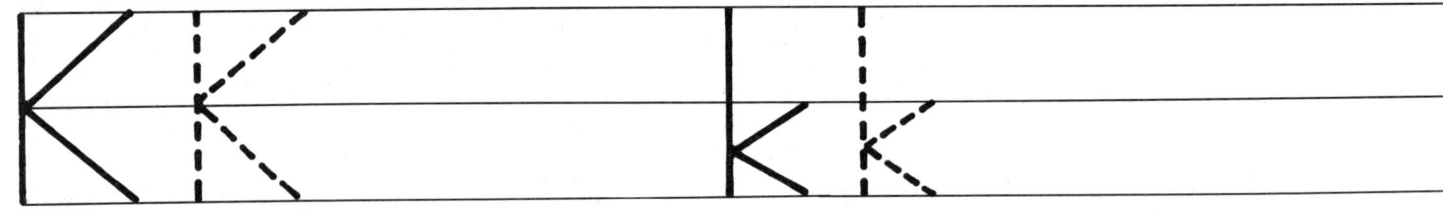

kangaroo

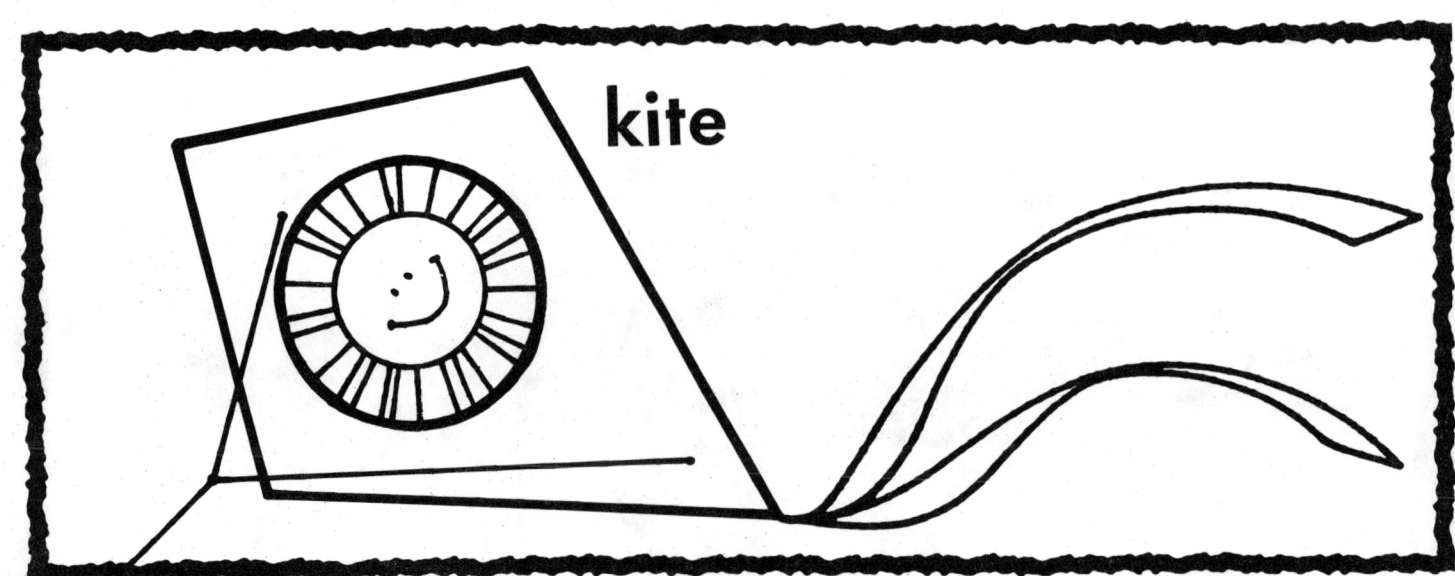

kite

The Alphabet
Letters of the Alphabet

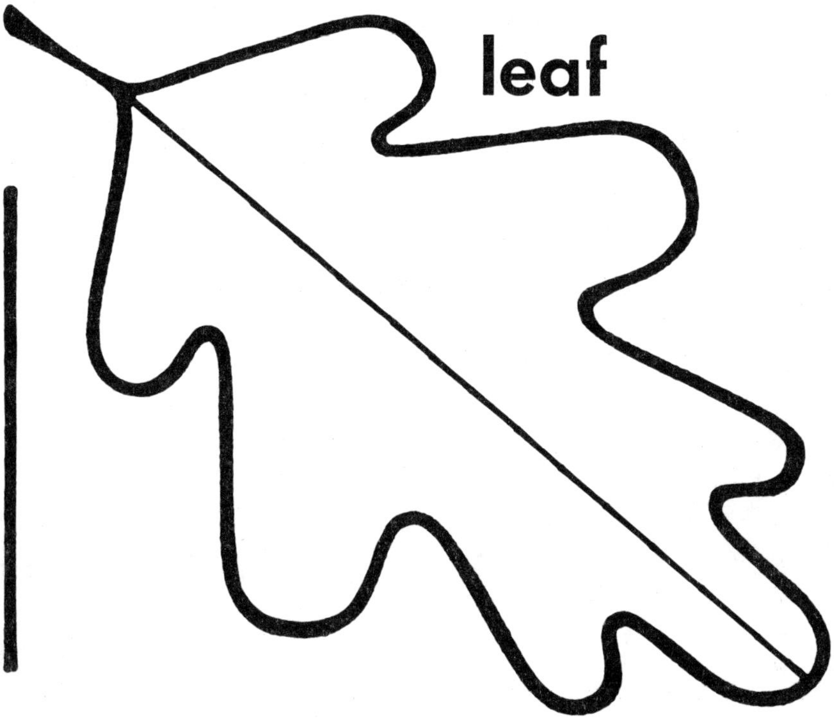

Name _____

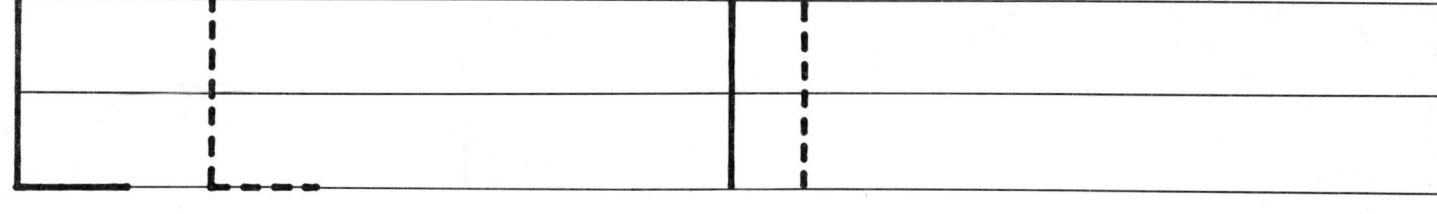

The Alphabet
Letters of the Alphabet

Name _____

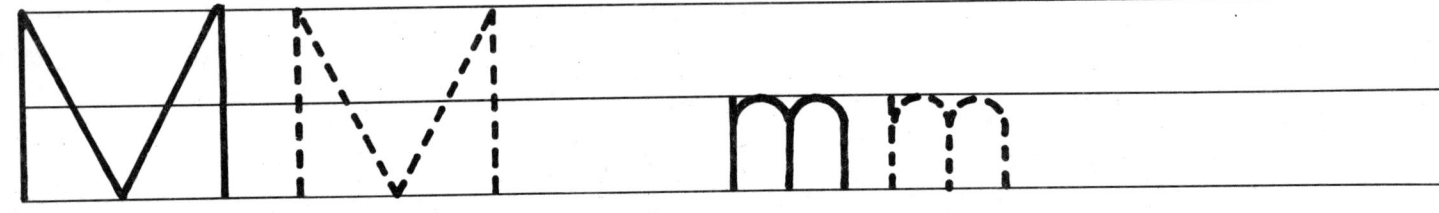

monkey

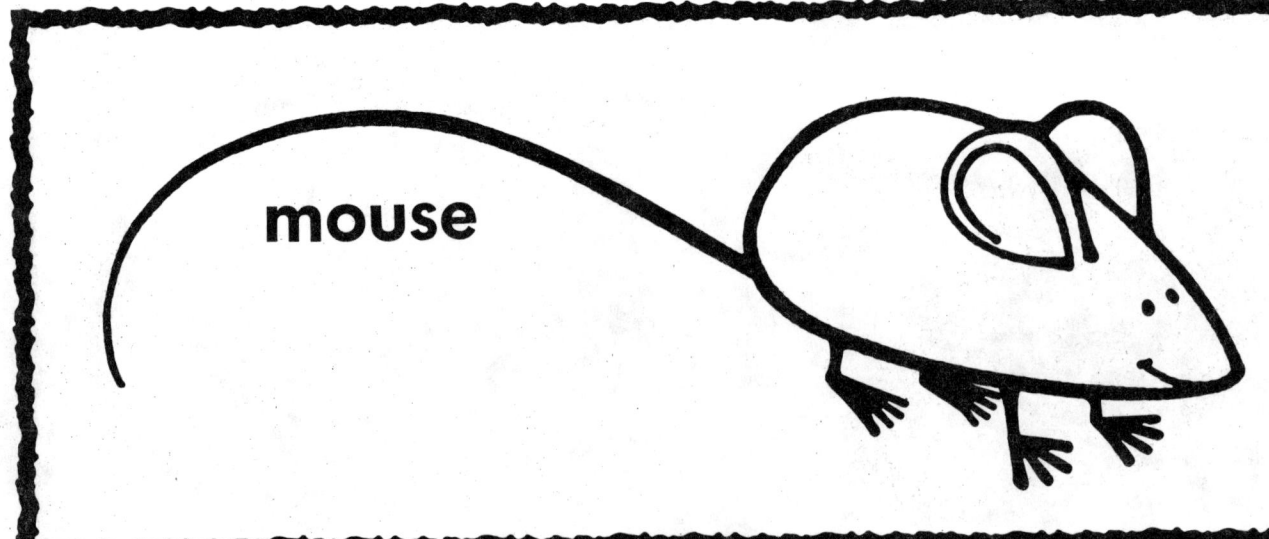

mouse

The Alphabet
Letters of the Alphabet

Name _____

nest

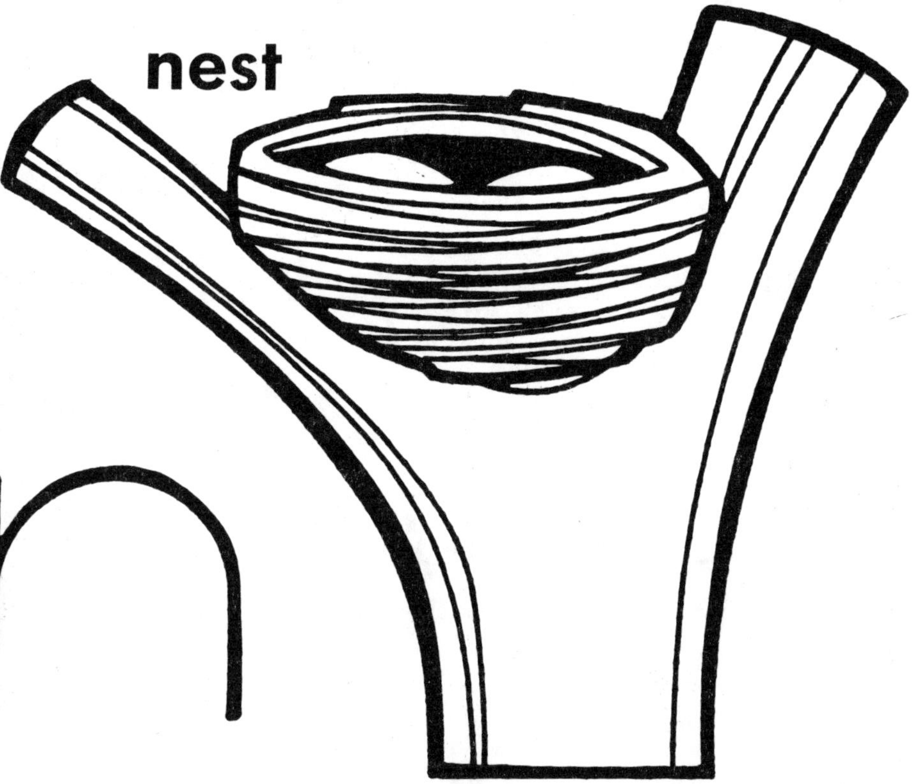

N n

N N n n

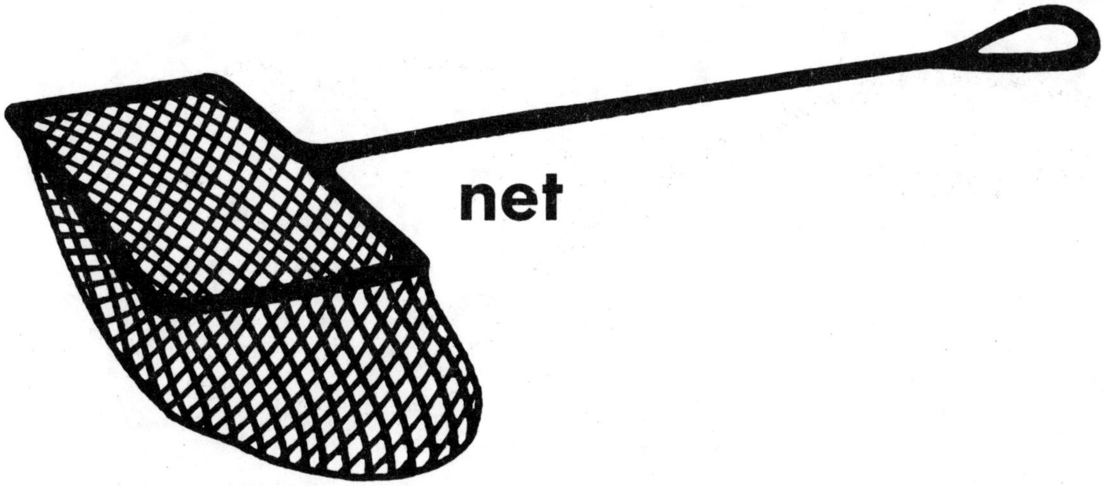

net

The Alphabet
Letters of the Alphabet

Name _____

owl

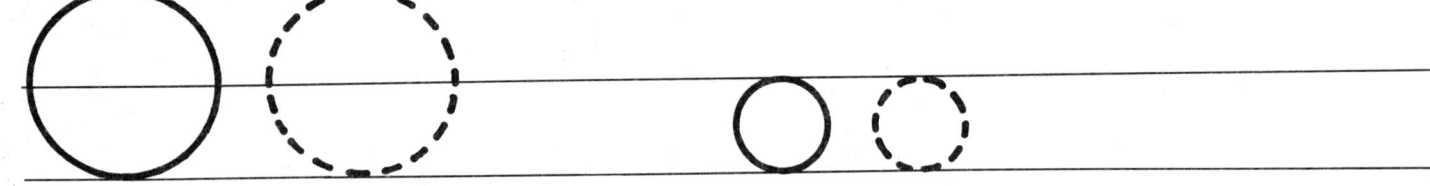

octopus

The Alphabet
Letters of the Alphabet

Name _____

Pp

pumpkin

pie

The Preschool Teacher's Pet
©1989–The Learning Works, Inc.

The Alphabet
Letters of the Alphabet

Name _____

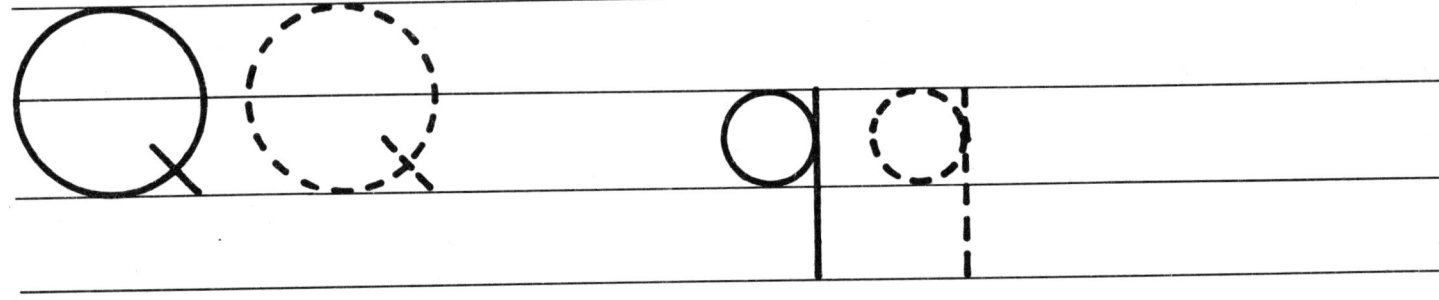

question marks

The Alphabet
Letters of the Alphabet

Name _____

rhinoceros

R R   r r

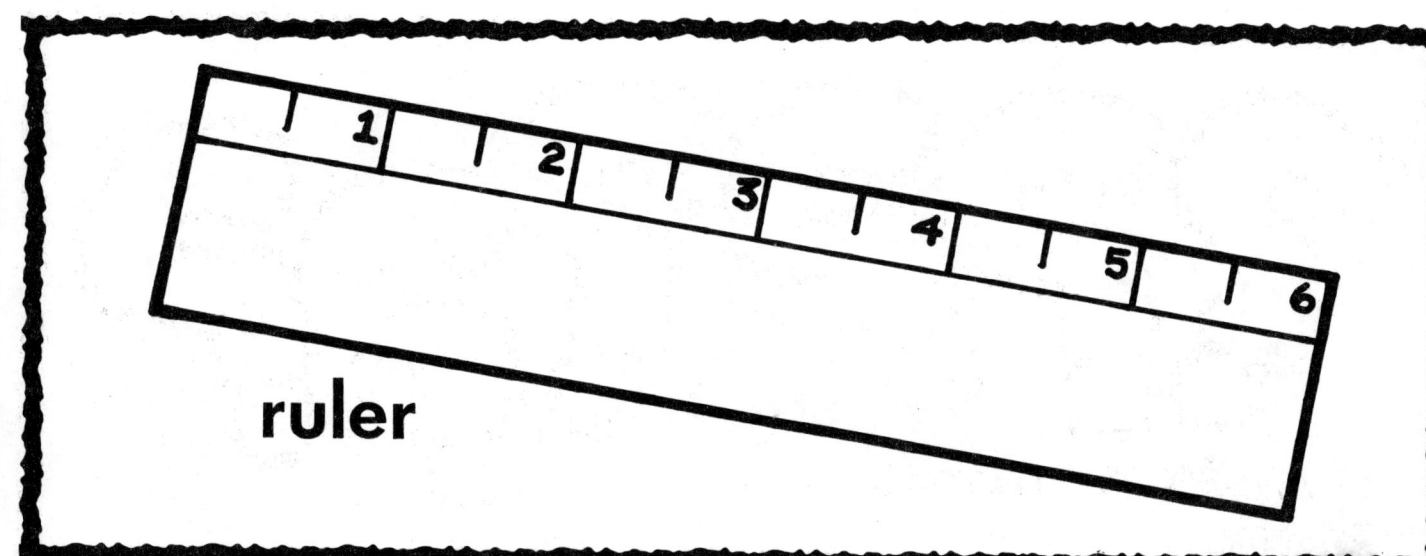

ruler

The Alphabet
Letters of the Alphabet

Name _____

snail

spider

The Alphabet
Letters of the Alphabet

Name _____

turtle

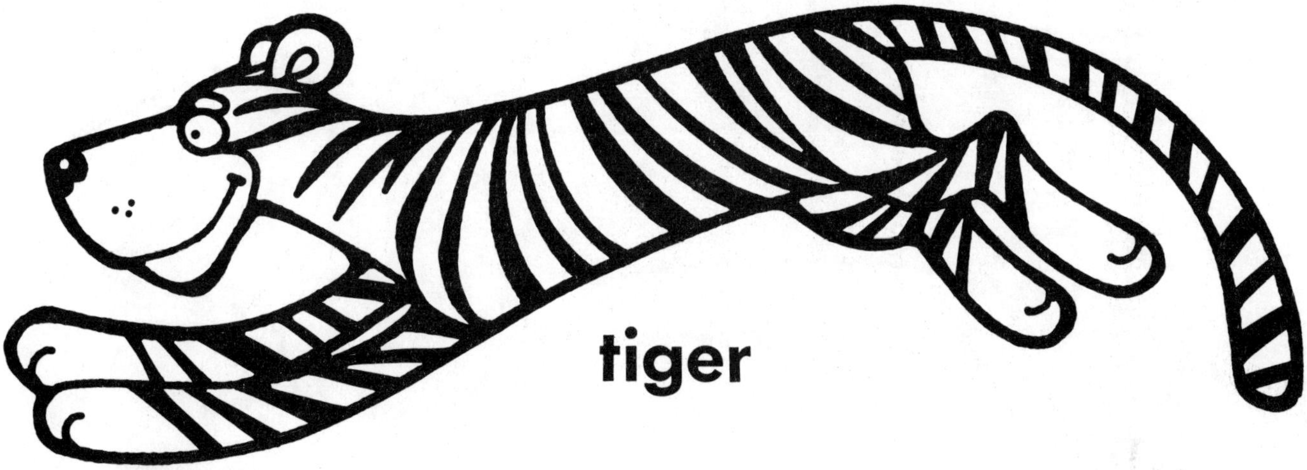

tiger

The Preschool Teacher's Pet
©1989–The Learning Works, Inc.

The Alphabet
Letters of the Alphabet

Name _____

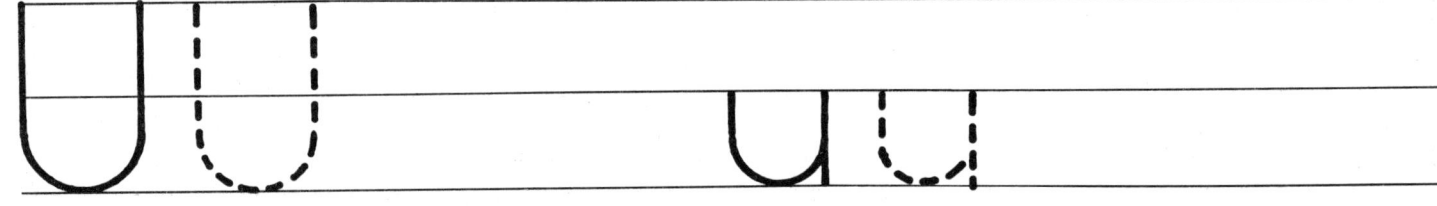

umbrella

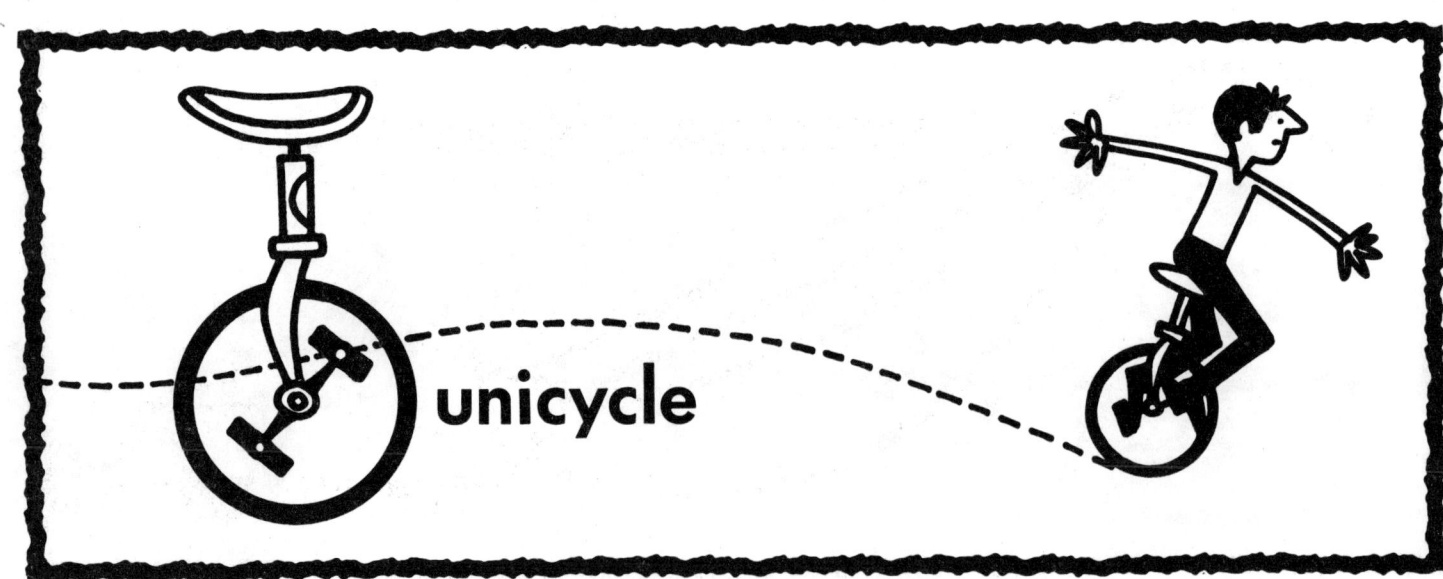

unicycle

The Alphabet
Letters of the Alphabet

Name _____

valentine

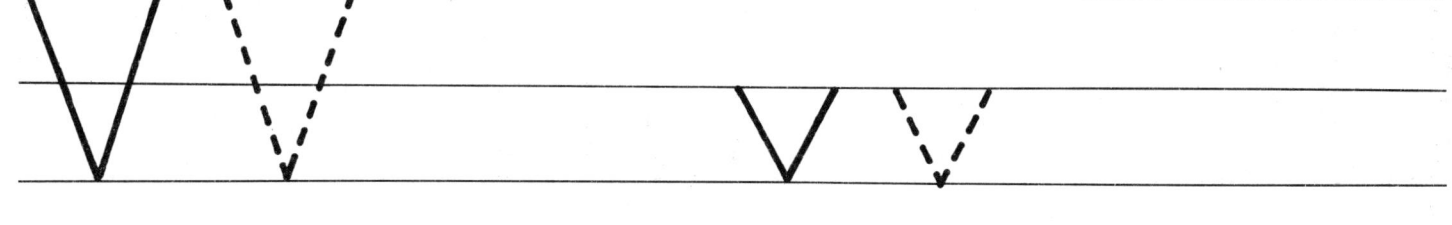

vacuum cleaner

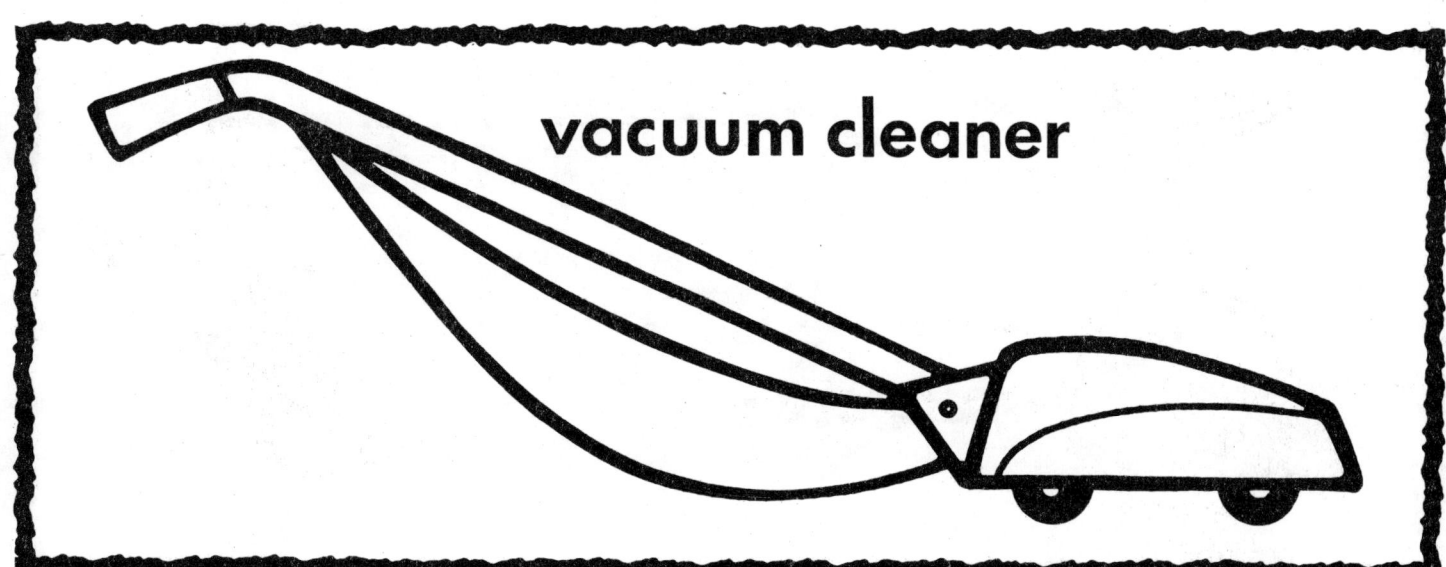

The Preschool Teacher's Pet
©1989—The Learning Works, Inc.

The Alphabet
Letters of the Alphabet

Name _____

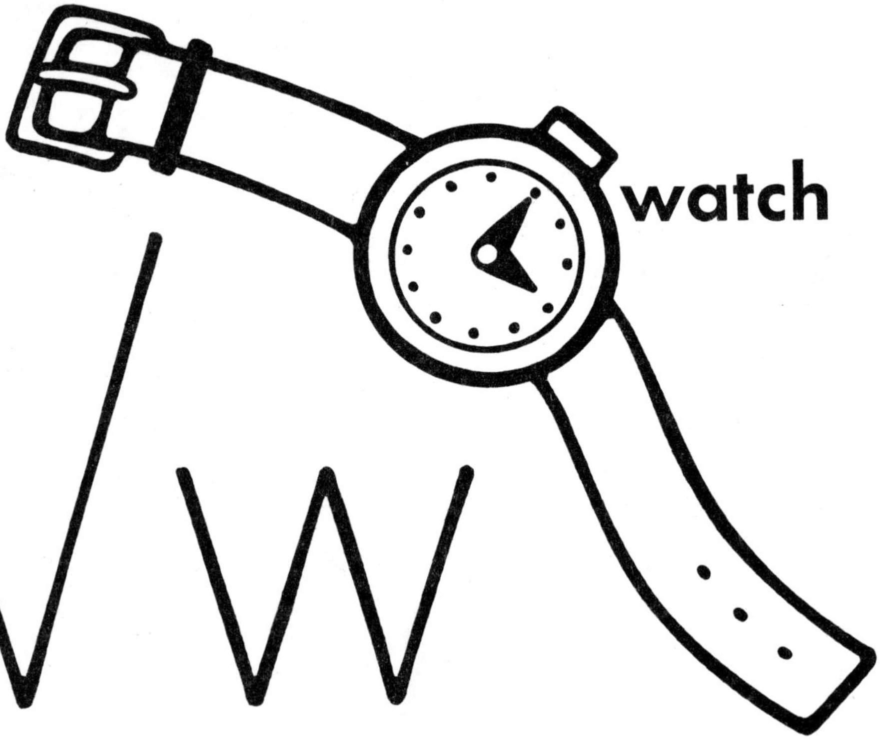

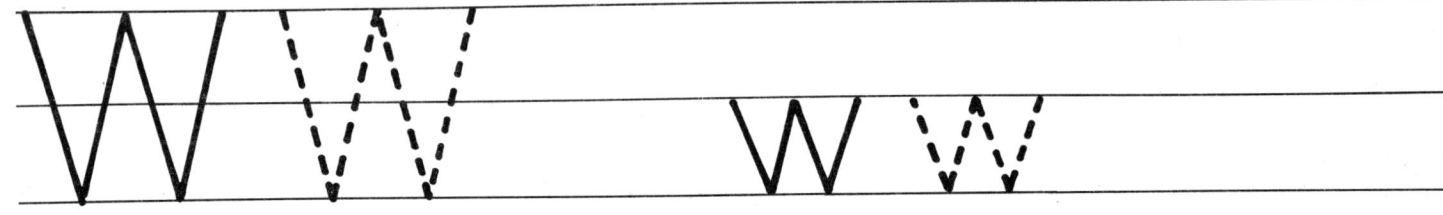

watch

whale

The Preschool Teacher's Pet
©1989–The Learning Works, Inc.

136

The Alphabet
Letters of the Alphabet

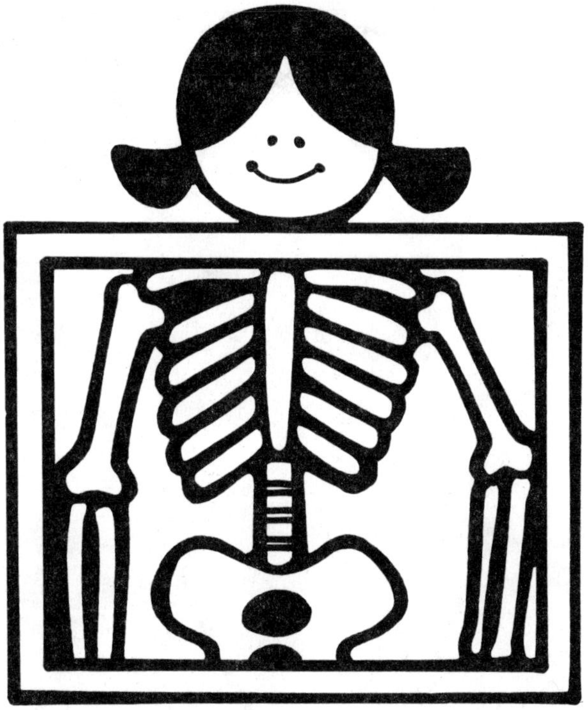

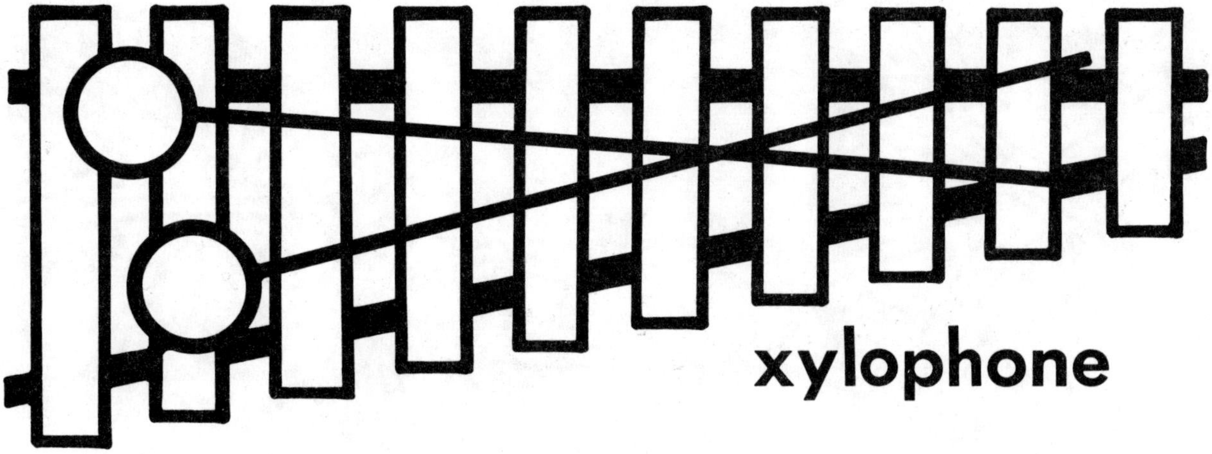

Name _____

X-ray

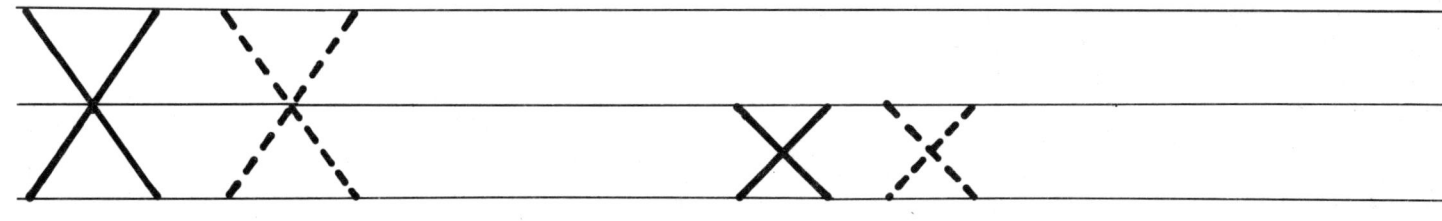

xylophone

The Alphabet
Letters of the Alphabet

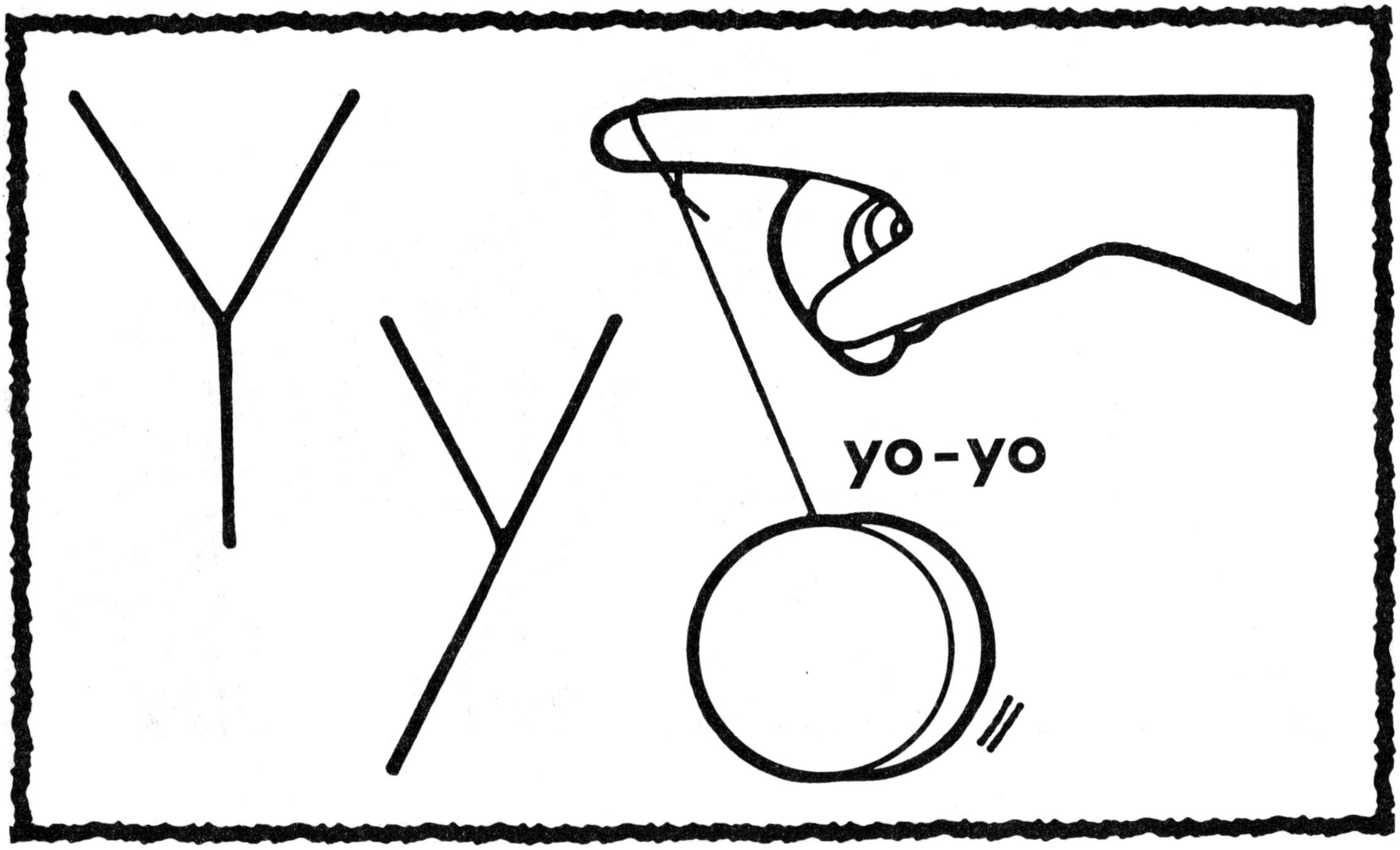

Name _____

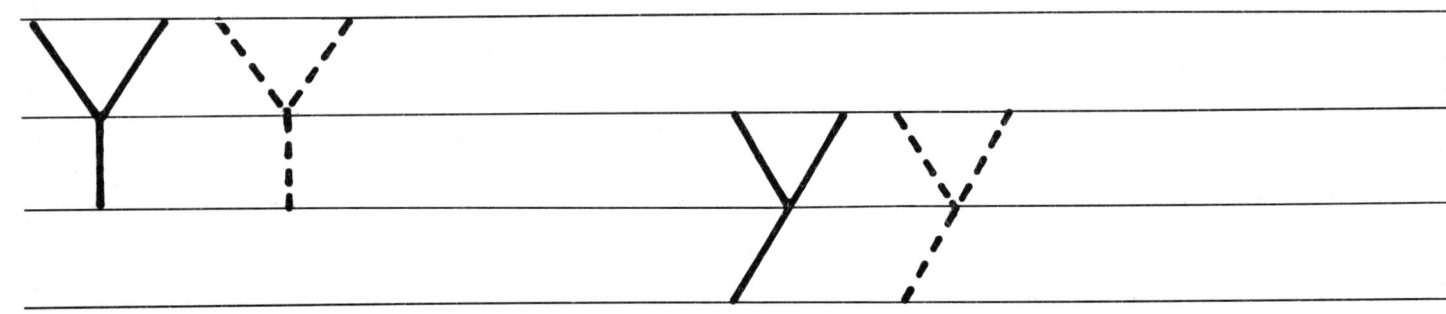

yo-yo

yarn

The Alphabet
Letters of the Alphabet

Name _____

zebra

zipper

The Alphabet   Name _____

Alphabet Chart

Aa Bb Cc Dd Ee
Ff Gg Hh Ii Jj Kk
Ll Mm Nn Oo Pp
Qq Rr Ss Tt Uu
Vv Ww Xx Yy Zz

Reading Readiness
Sequencing

Name _____

What's Next?

Color the picture that comes next.

Reading Readiness
Sequencing

Name _____

String a Bead

Color the bead that comes next.

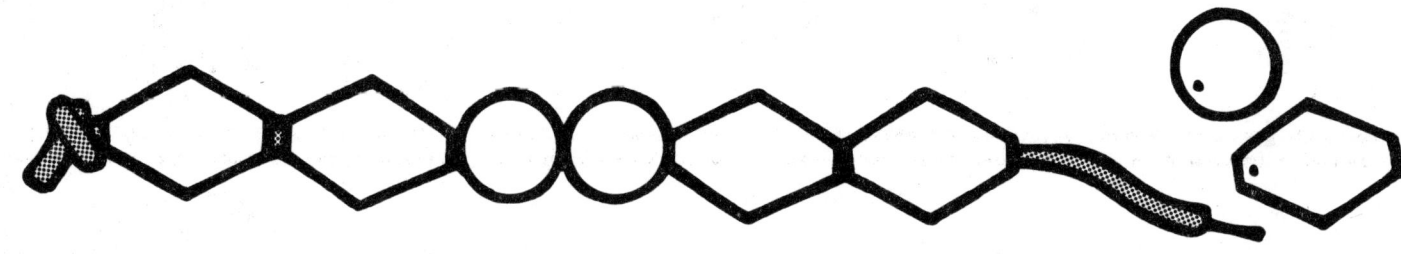

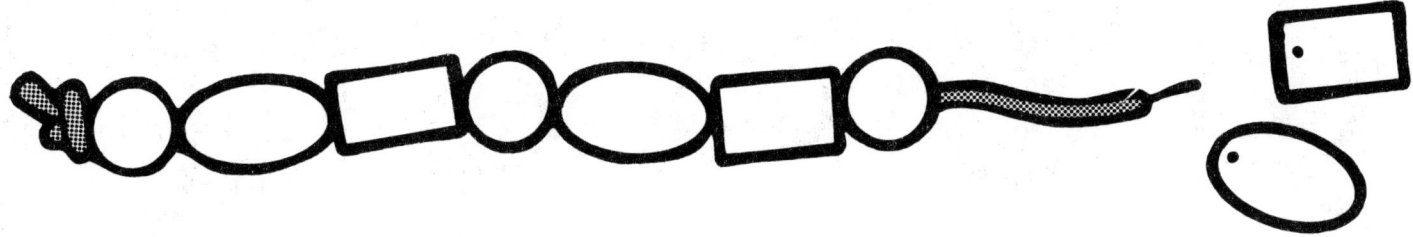

Reading Readiness
Sequencing

Blow a Bubble

Cut out the pictures and paste them in the squares where they belong.

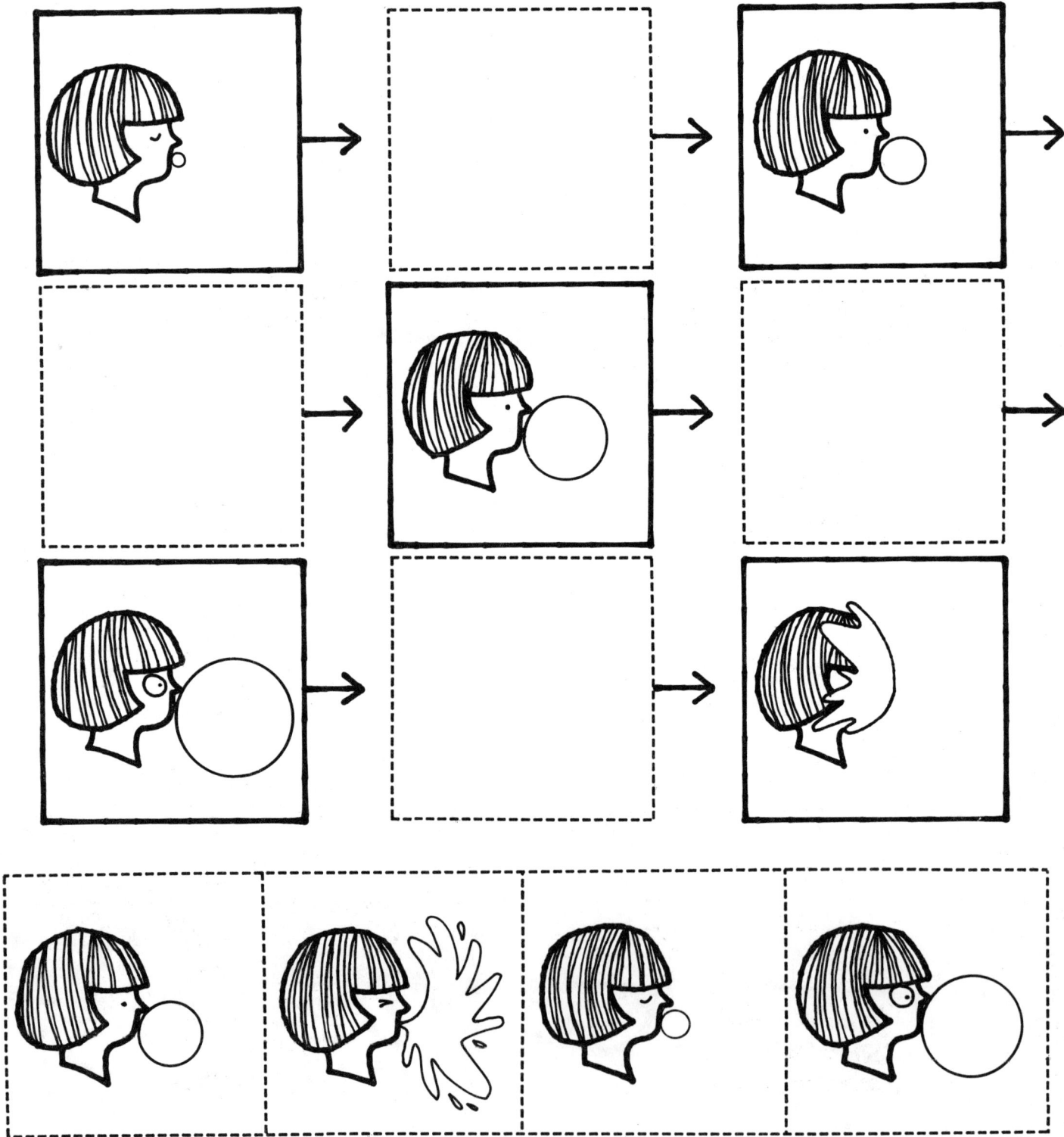

Reading Readiness
Sequencing

Name _____

Watermelon Time

Draw a line from the first picture in this sequence to the second picture. Then continue to connect the pictures in order.

The Preschool Teacher's Pet
©1989–The Learning Works, Inc.

Reading Readiness
Sequencing

Name _____

Draw a Dinosaur

Paste the numbers in the squares to show the first, second, third, and fourth steps in drawing a dinosaur.

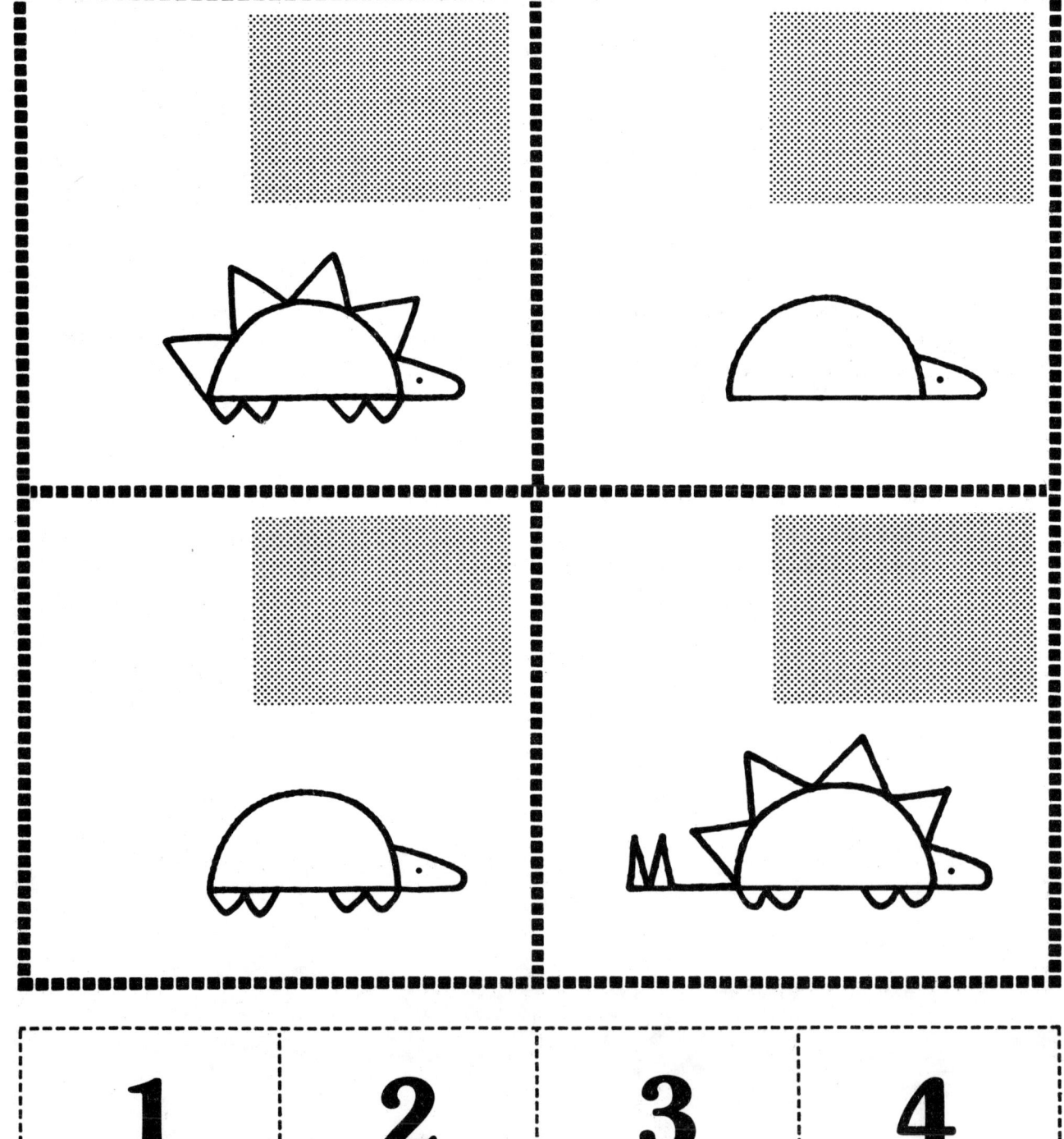

Reading Readiness
Sequencing

Name _____

Draw an Alligator

Paste the numbers in the squares to show the first, second, third, and fourth steps in drawing an alligator.

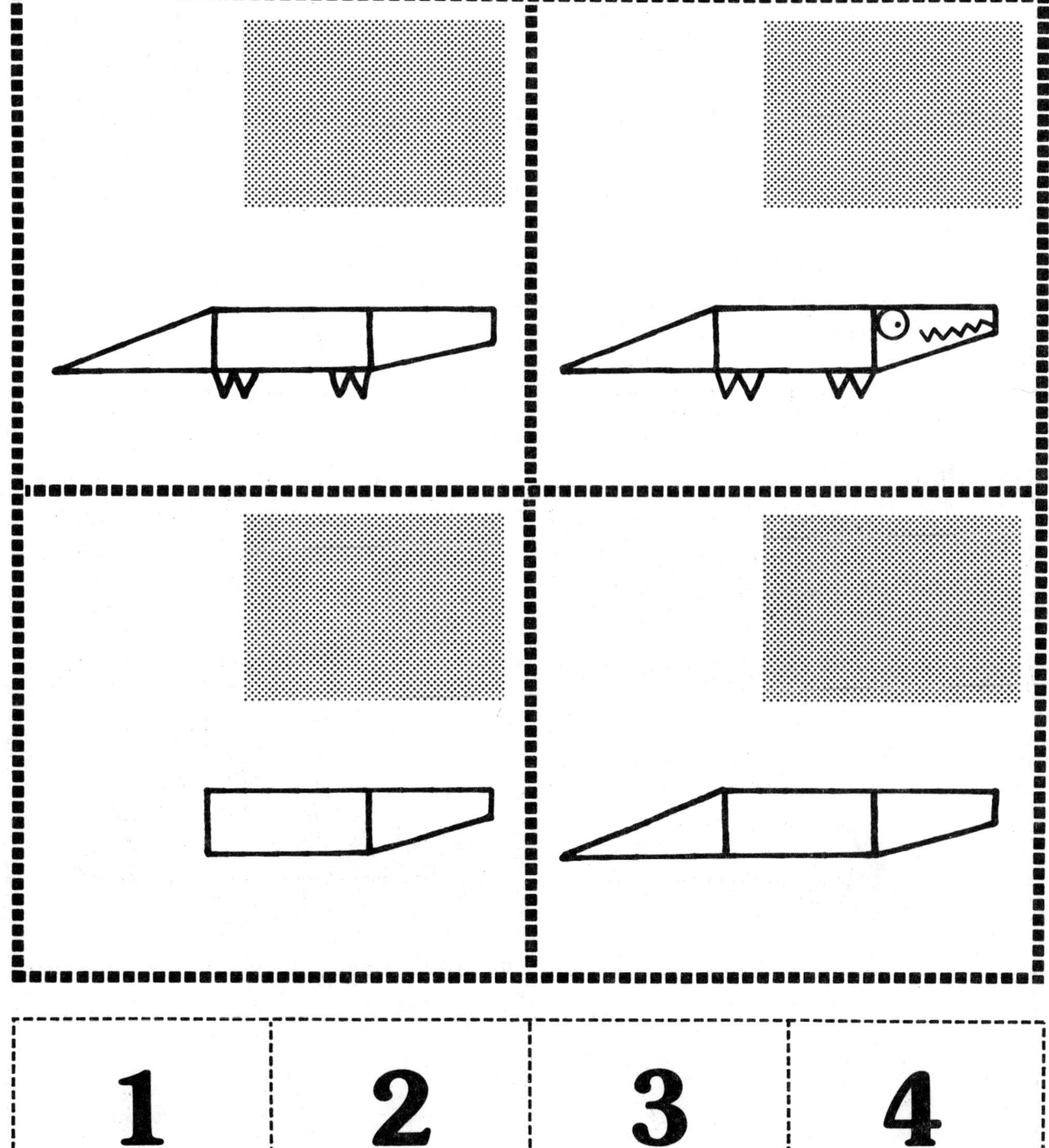

Reading Readiness
Sequencing

Name _____

Hatching Chick

Mark these pictures to show how a chick hatches. Draw one dot in the picture that shows the first thing that happens. Then draw two dots in the second picture of the sequence, three in the third, and four in the fourth.

Reading Readiness
Sequencing

Name _____

Decorate a Cookie

Number the steps in decorating the cookie. Circle number one for the first step, number two for the second step, and so on.

1 2 3 4 5 6   1 2 3 4 5 6   1 2 3 4 5 6

1 2 3 4 5 6   1 2 3 4 5 6   1 2 3 4 5 6

The Preschool Teacher's Pet
©1989–The Learning Works, Inc.

Reading Readiness
Classifying

Name _____

Hot or Cold

Cut and paste the pictures of things that are **hot** and things that are **cold**.

The Preschool Teacher's Pet
©1989–The Learning Works, Inc.
150

Reading Readiness
Classifying

Name _____

Front or Back

Cut out the pictures. Paste those that show the **fronts** of things in the top row. Paste those that show the **backs** of things in the bottom row.

Front

Back

The Preschool Teacher's Pet
©1989–The Learning Works, Inc.

Reading Readiness
Classifying

Name _____

Fruit or Vegetable?

Cut out the five fruits and paste them in the bowl.

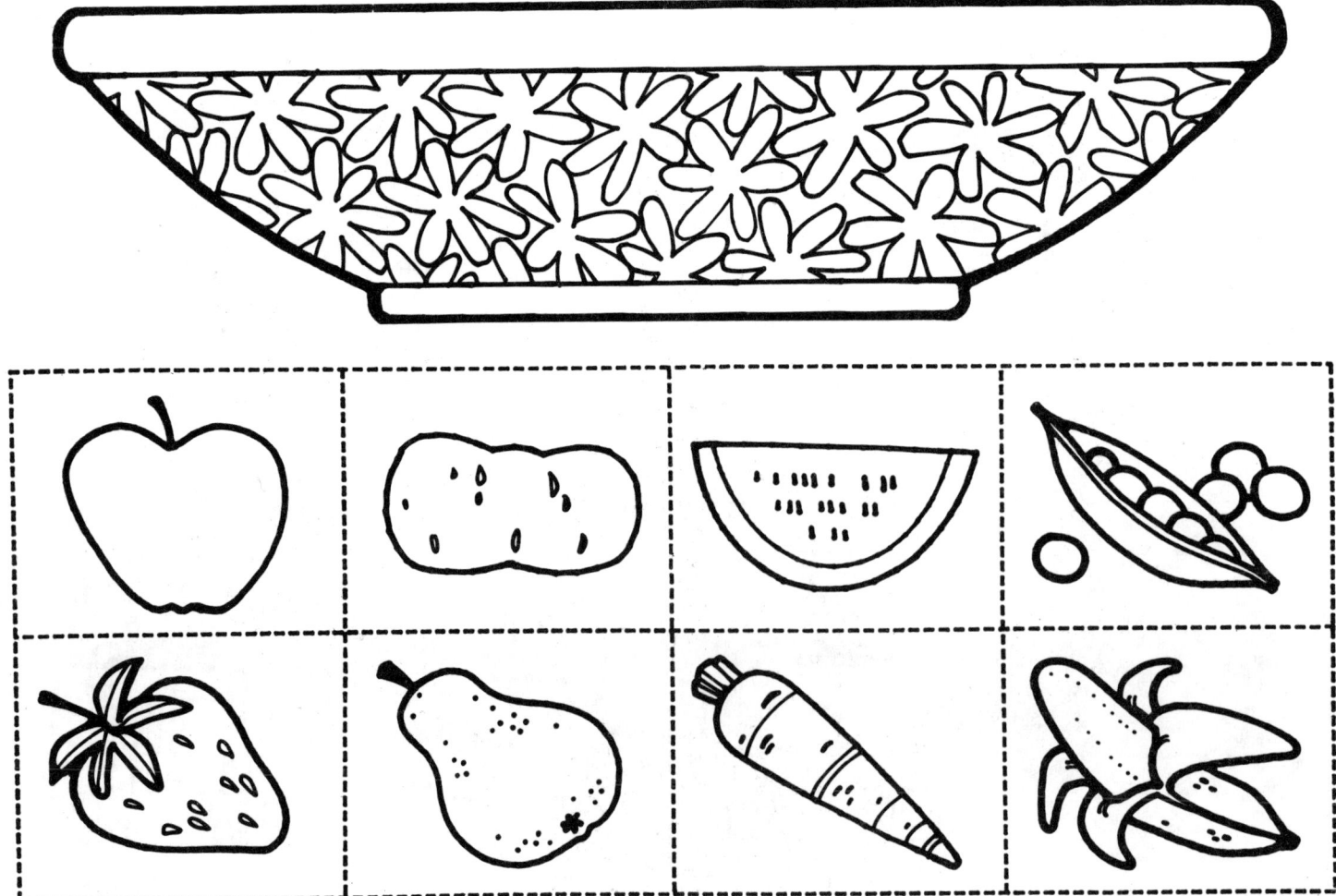

The Preschool Teacher's Pet
©1989–The Learning Works, Inc.

Reading Readiness
Classifying

Name _____

Letters and Numbers

Find and color the six balls with numbers.

The Preschool Teacher's Pet
©1989–The Learning Works, Inc.

Reading Readiness
Classifying

Name _____

Hard or Soft

Cut and paste the pictures of things that are **hard** and things that are **soft**.

The Preschool Teacher's Pet
©1989—The Learning Works, Inc.

154

Reading Readiness
Classifying

Name _____

Land, Water, or Air

Draw a line from each animal to the place where it likes to be most of the time.

Reading Readiness
Classifying

Name _____

Good to Eat

Cut out the four pictures of things that are good to eat. Paste the pictures in the basket.

The Preschool Teacher's Pet
©1989—The Learning Works, Inc.

Reading Readiness
Classifying

Name _____

Shapes to Color

◯ purple   ☐ red   △ green   ☐ blue

The Preschool Teacher's Pet
©1989—The Learning Works, Inc.

Reading Readiness
Perception

Name _____

The Shoe Shop

Cut out the shoes and paste each one on the shelf where it belongs.

Butterflies

Color the butterflies that are flying **to** the flower yellow. Color the butterflies that are flying **away from** the flower orange.

Reading Readiness
Perception

Name _____

Find the Fish

In each row, color the fish in the box and the two other fish that are exactly like it.

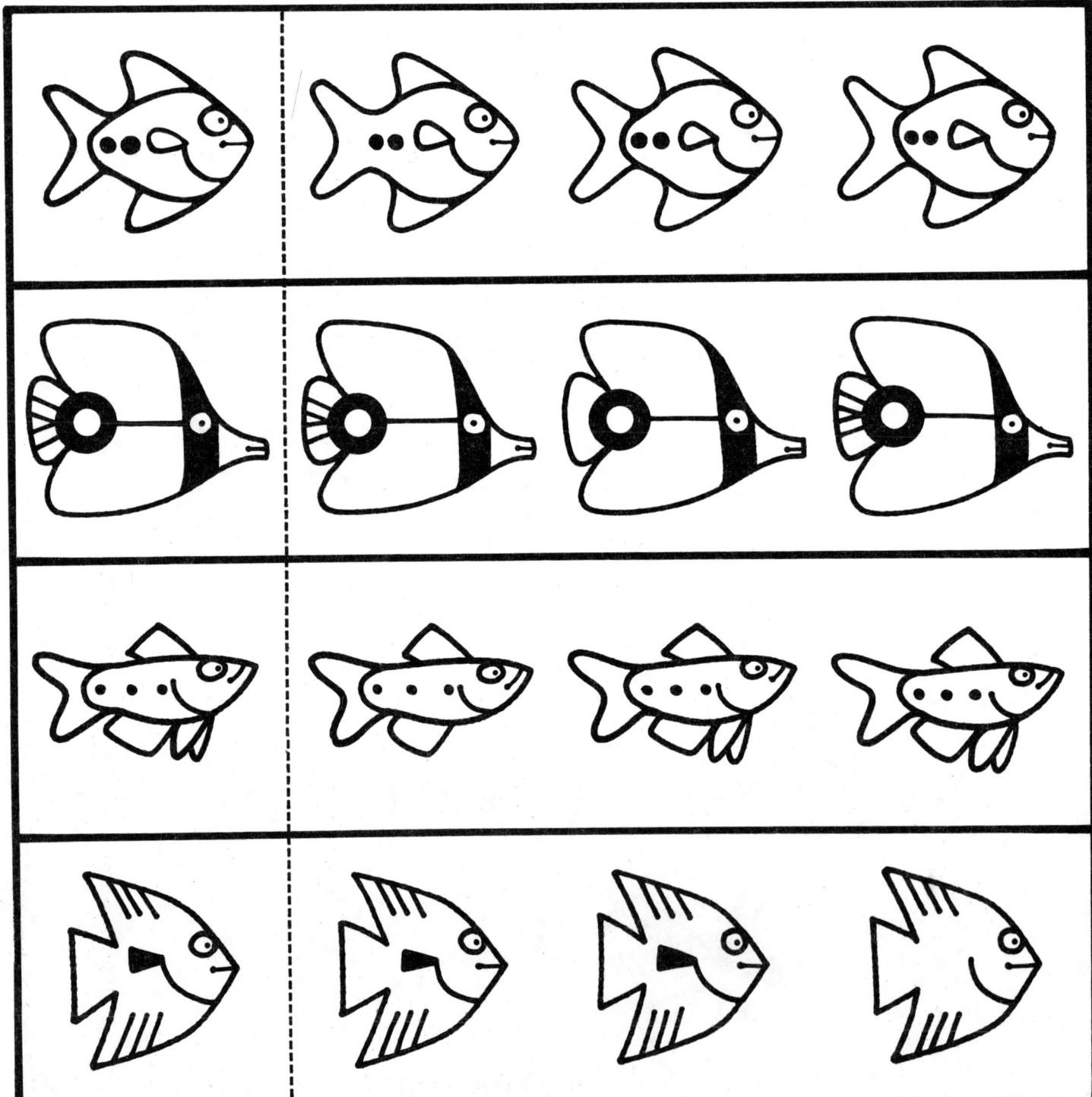

Letters and Leaves

Color orange all of the leaves with the letter **d** on them. Color green all of the leaves with the letter **b** on them.

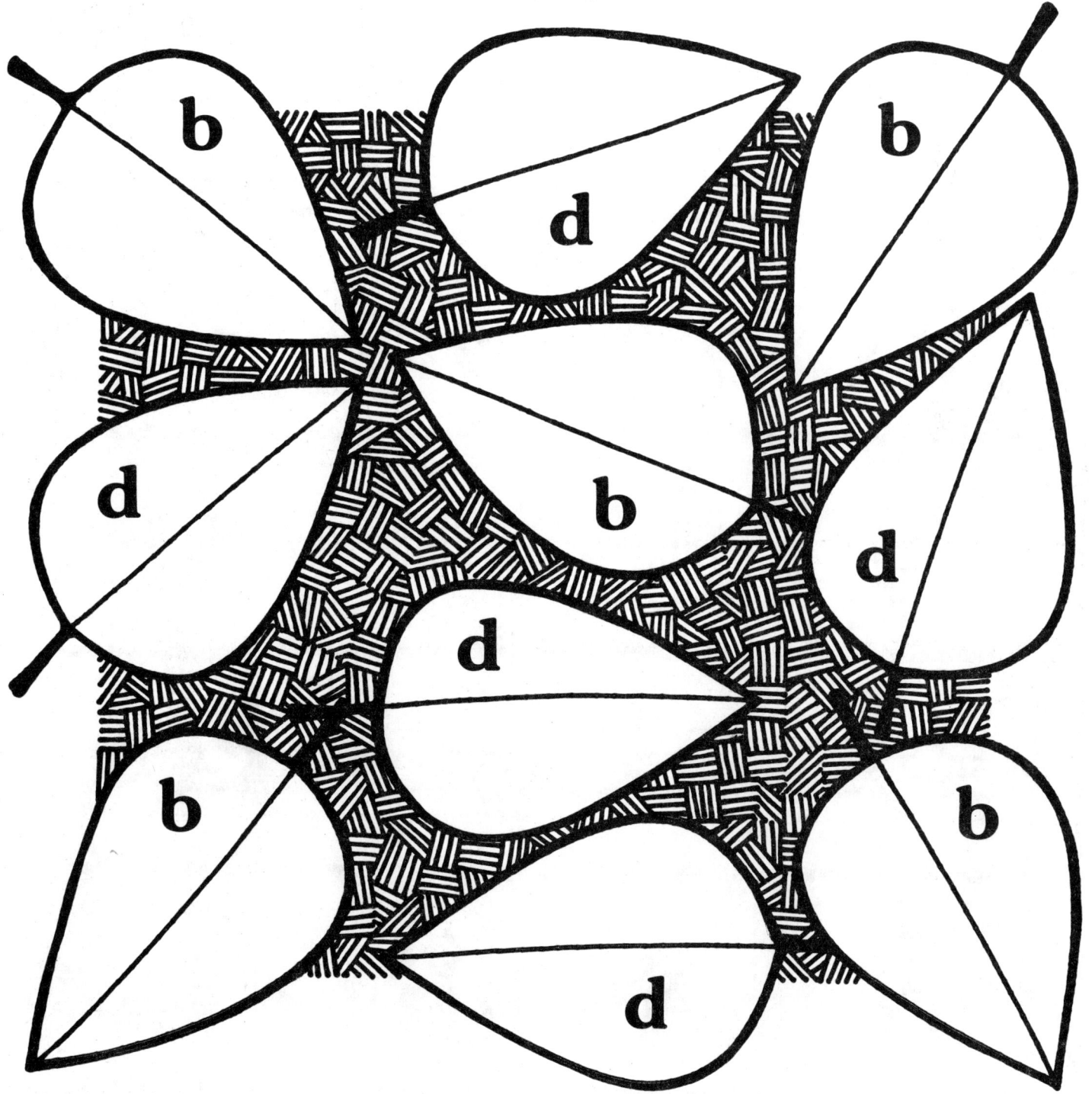

Reading Readiness
Perception

Name _____

Find the Bug

One bug in each row is different from the others. Find the bug that is different and color it.

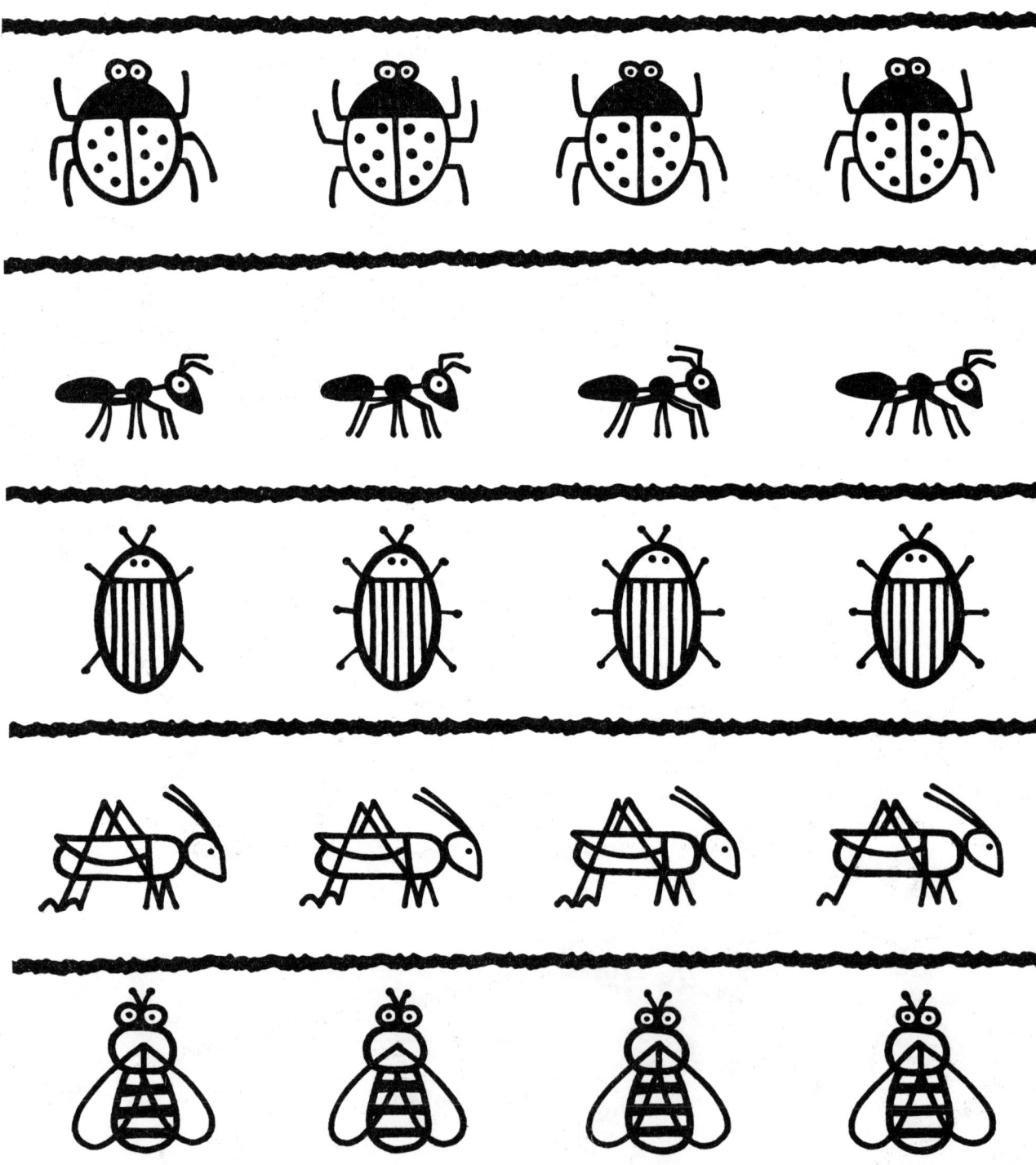

Reading Readiness
Perception

Name _____

Spot-a-saurus

Find the six spots with the letter **n** and color them yellow.

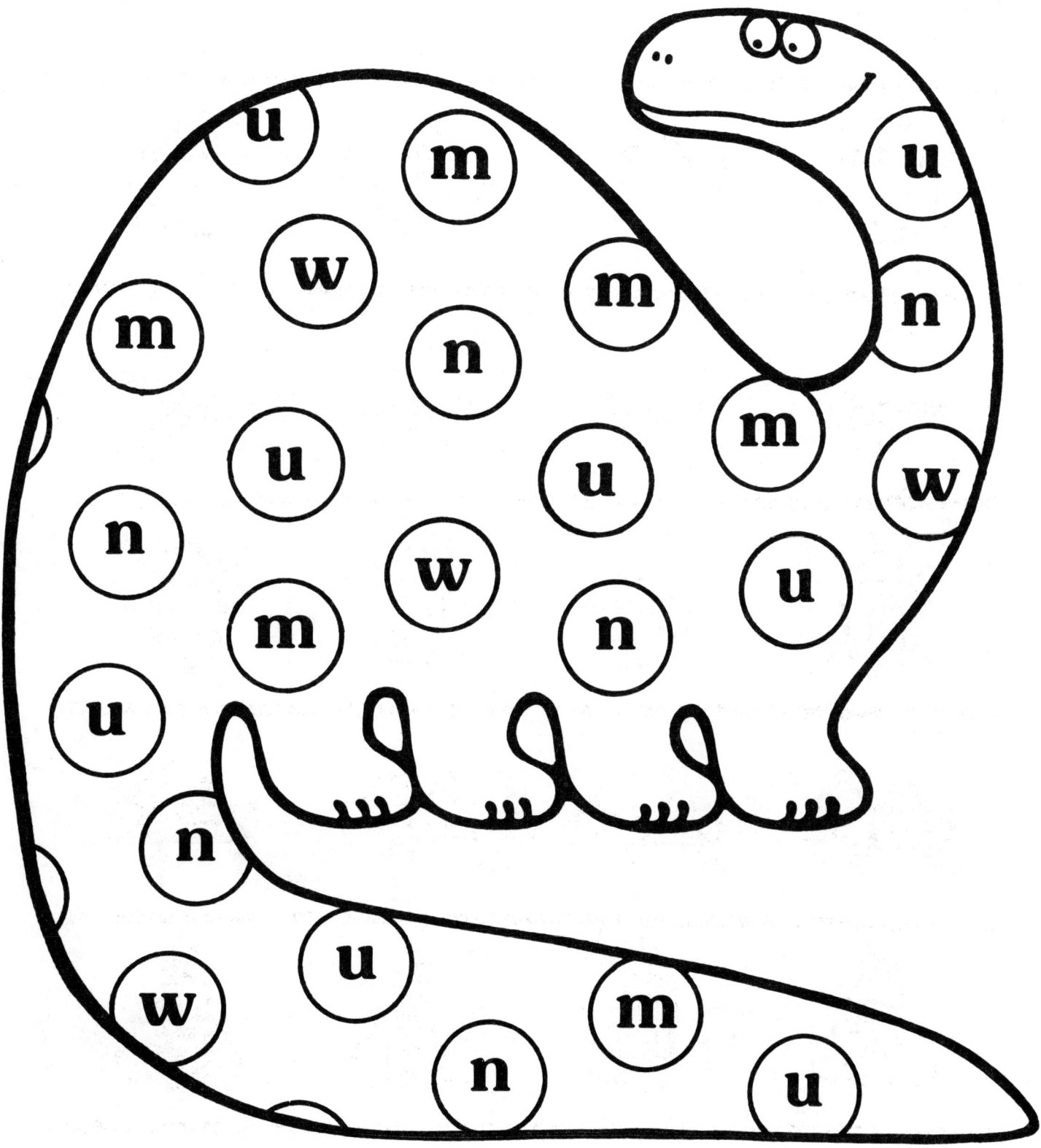

The Preschool Teacher's Pet
©1989—The Learning Works, Inc.
163

Reading Readiness
Perception

Name _____

Shadow Search

Draw a line from each dinosaur to its shadow.

Triangle Tricks

Cut out the triangles. Use them to copy these designs.

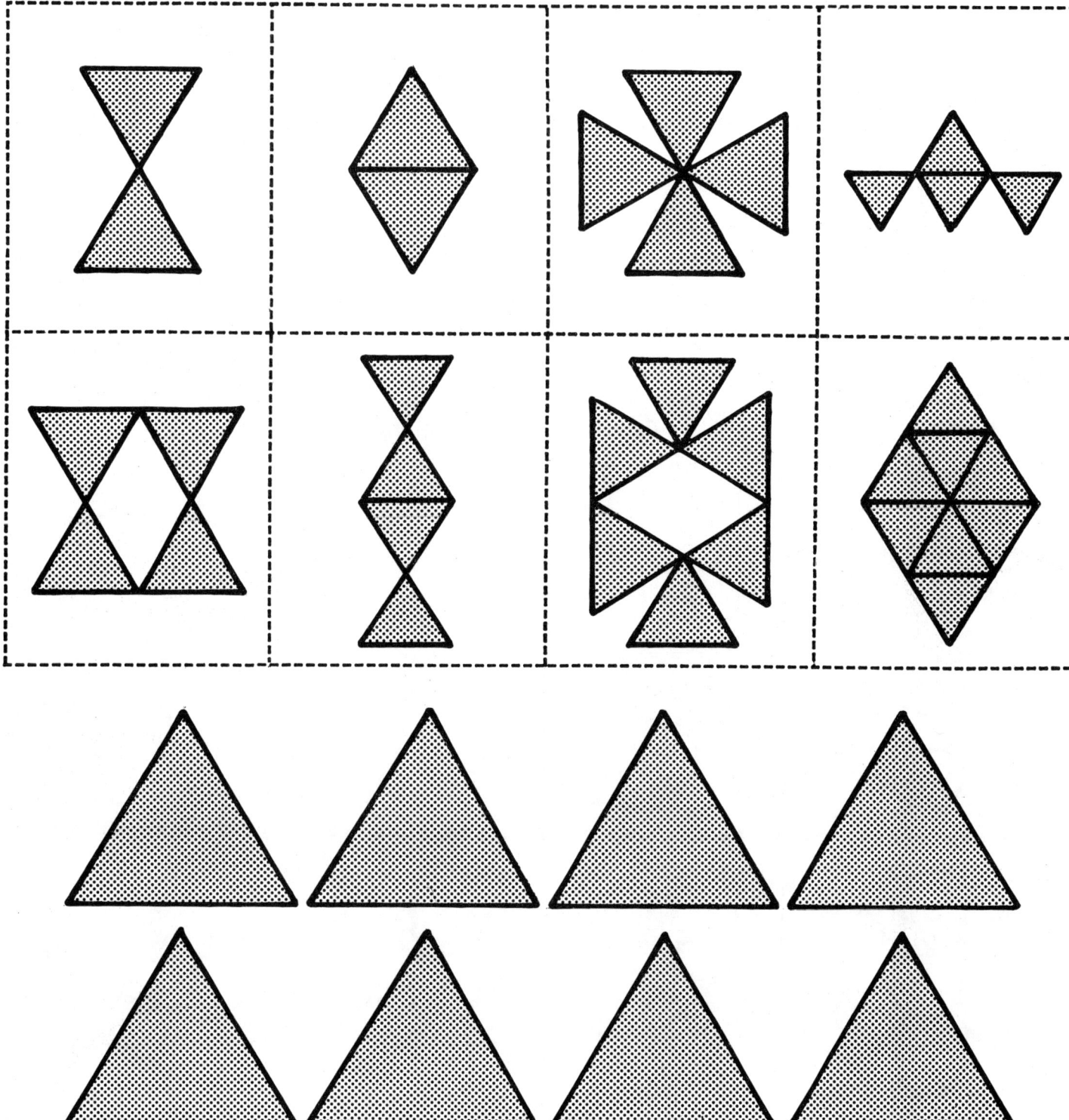

Reading Readiness
Matching

Name _____

Same Size

Color the picture that is the same size as the one on the left.

Reading Readiness
Matching

Name _____

Find the Shadow

Draw lines to connect the animals with their shadows.

The Preschool Teacher's Pet
©1989–The Learning Works, Inc.

Reading Readiness
Matching

Name _____

Same Shape

Color the picture that is the same shape as the one on the left.

The Preschool Teacher's Pet
©1989–The Learning Works, Inc.
168

Reading Readiness
Matching

Name _____

Home Sweet Home

Connect the pictures of the animals with their homes.

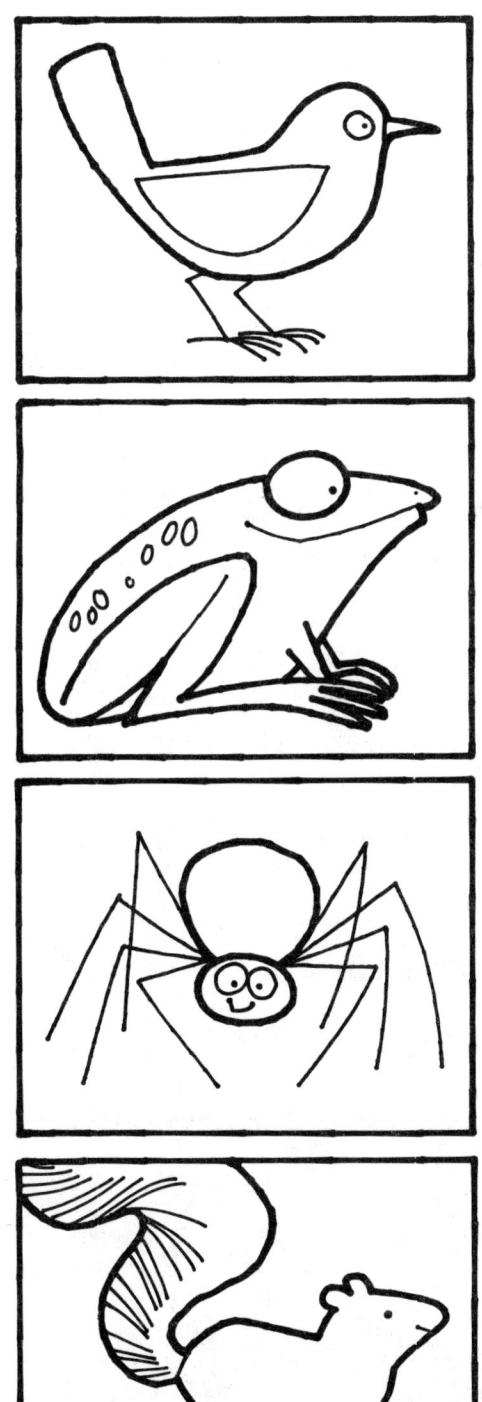
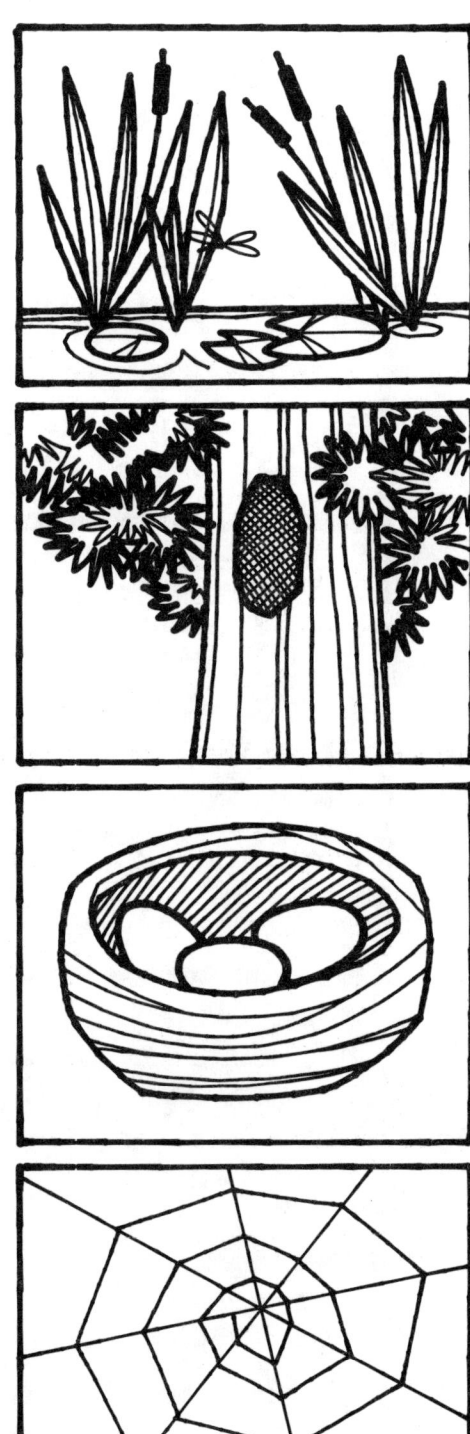

Reading Readiness
Matching

Name _____

At the Table

Cut out the pictures. Paste each one next to the picture of the food that goes with it.

The Preschool Teacher's Pet
©1989–The Learning Works, Inc.
170

Reading Readiness
Matching

Name _____

In the Bathroom

Cut out the pictures of things that are found in the bathroom. Paste them next to the pictures that show where they are used.

The Preschool Teacher's Pet
©1989–The Learning Works, Inc.

Reading Readiness
Matching

Name _____

Choose the Shoes

Cut out the shoes. Paste each pair next to the child who needs that kind of shoes.

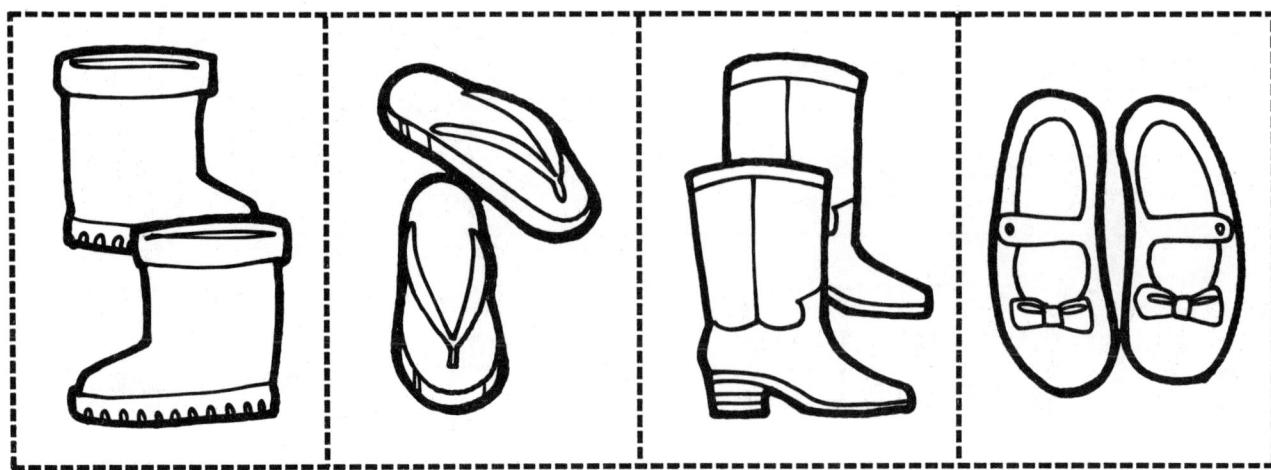

Reading Readiness
Matching

Name _____

Tools and Things

Cut out the pictures and paste each one next to the tool that is used with it.

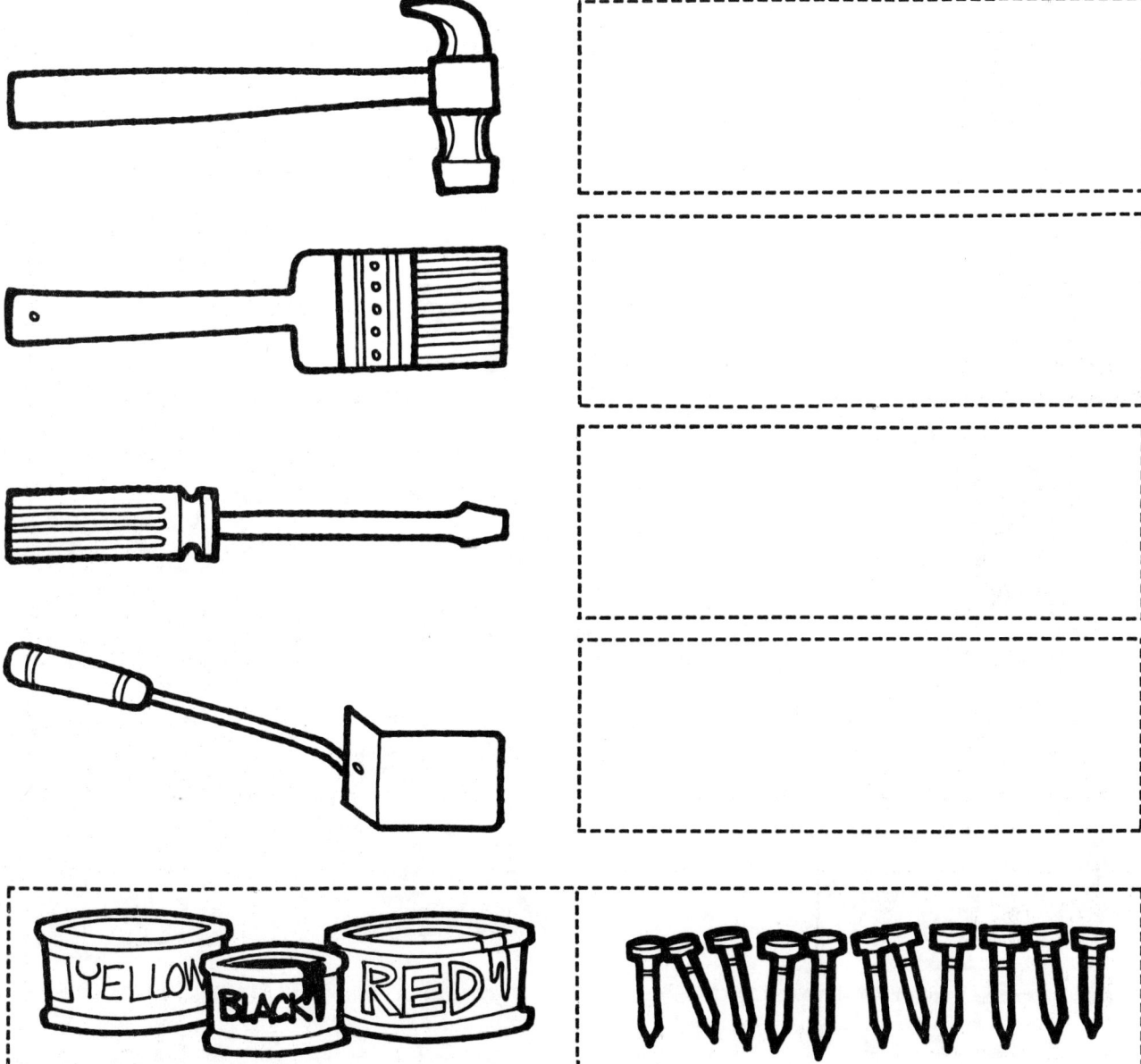

The Preschool Teacher's Pet
©1989—The Learning Works, Inc.

173

Reading Readiness
Rhyming

Name _____

Rhyme Time

Color the two pictures in each row that rhyme.

Reading Readiness
Rhyming

Name _____

Rhyme Time

Cut out the pictures of things that rhyme and paste them in the squares where they belong.

The Preschool Teacher's Pet
©1989—The Learning Works, Inc.

Reading Readiness
Rhyming

Name _____

Rhyme Time

Color the two pictures in each row that rhyme.

Reading Readiness
Rhyming

Name _____

Rhyme Time

Cut out the pictures of things that rhyme and paste them in the square where they belong.

The Preschool Teacher's Pet
©1989–The Learning Works, Inc.

Reading Readiness
Rhyming

Name _____

Rhyme Time

Color the two pictures in each row that rhyme.

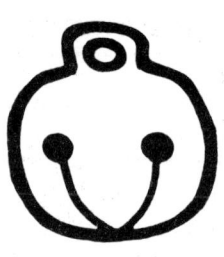 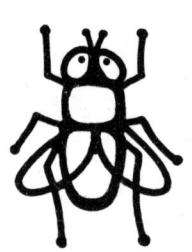 

Reading Readiness
Rhyming

Name _____

Rhyme Time

Color the two pictures in each row that rhyme.

The Preschool Teacher's Pet
©1989—The Learning Works, Inc.

Reading Readiness
Rhyming

Name _____

Rhyme Time

Cut out the pictures. Paste each one next to the picture with which it rhymes.

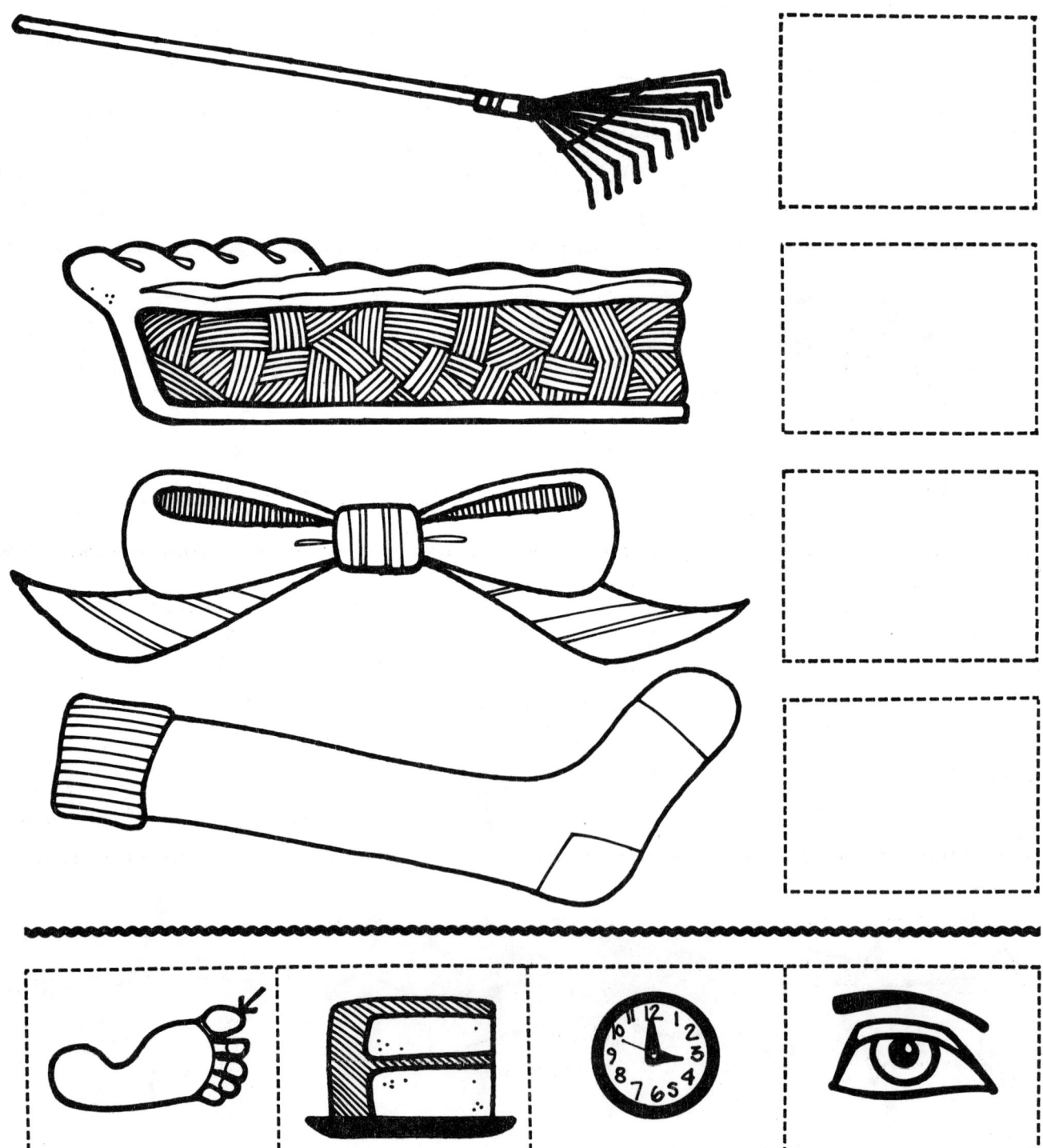

The Preschool Teacher's Pet
©1989–The Learning Works, Inc.
180

Rhyme Time

Color the two pictures in each row that rhyme.

Reading Readiness
Motor Skills

Name _____

On the Move

Connect each picture to a stop sign by tracing the line from left to right.

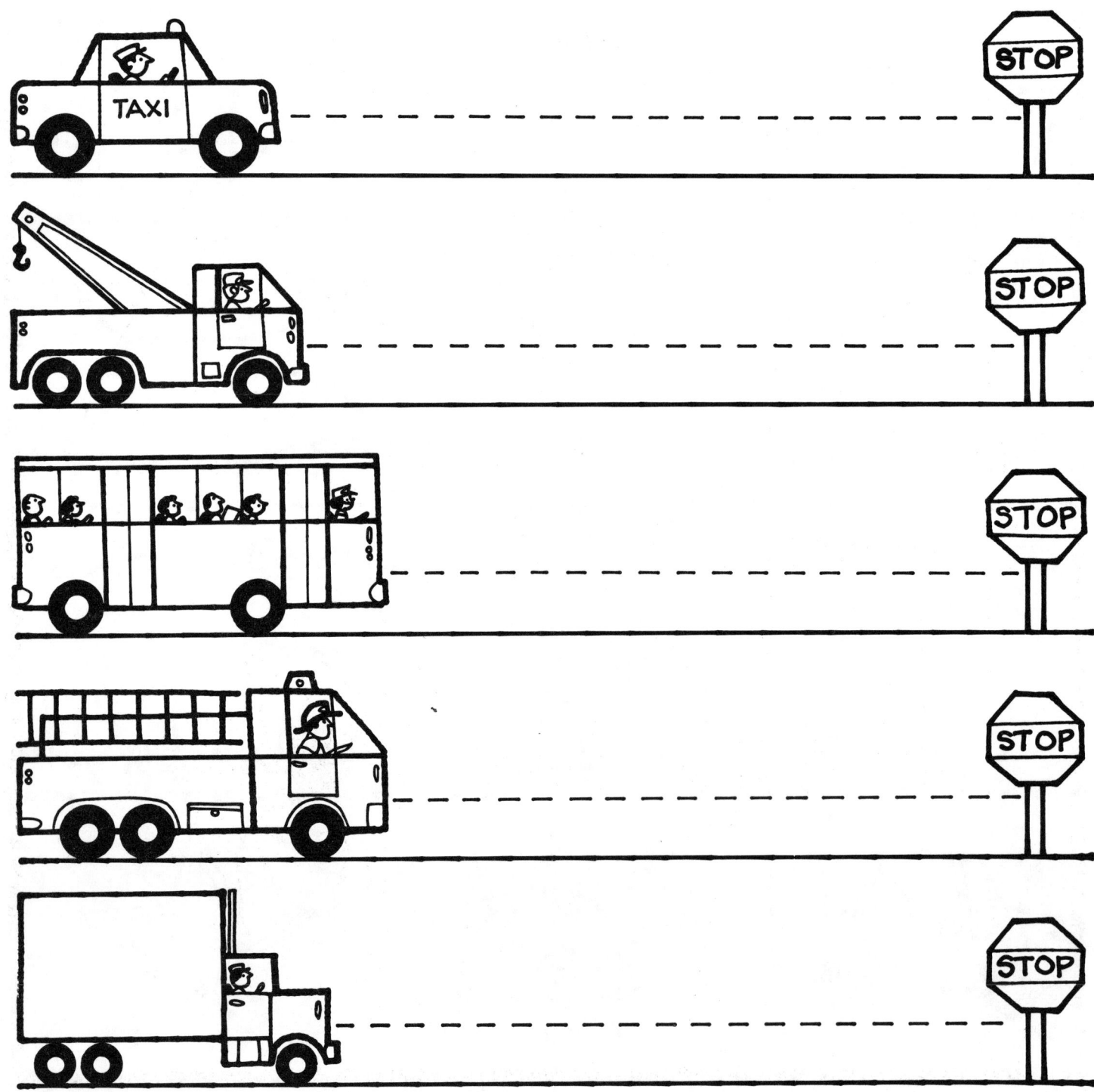

The Preschool Teacher's Pet
©1989–The Learning Works, Inc.

Reading Readiness
Motor Skills

Name _____

Weave a Web

Help the spider weave her web by tracing the dotted lines.

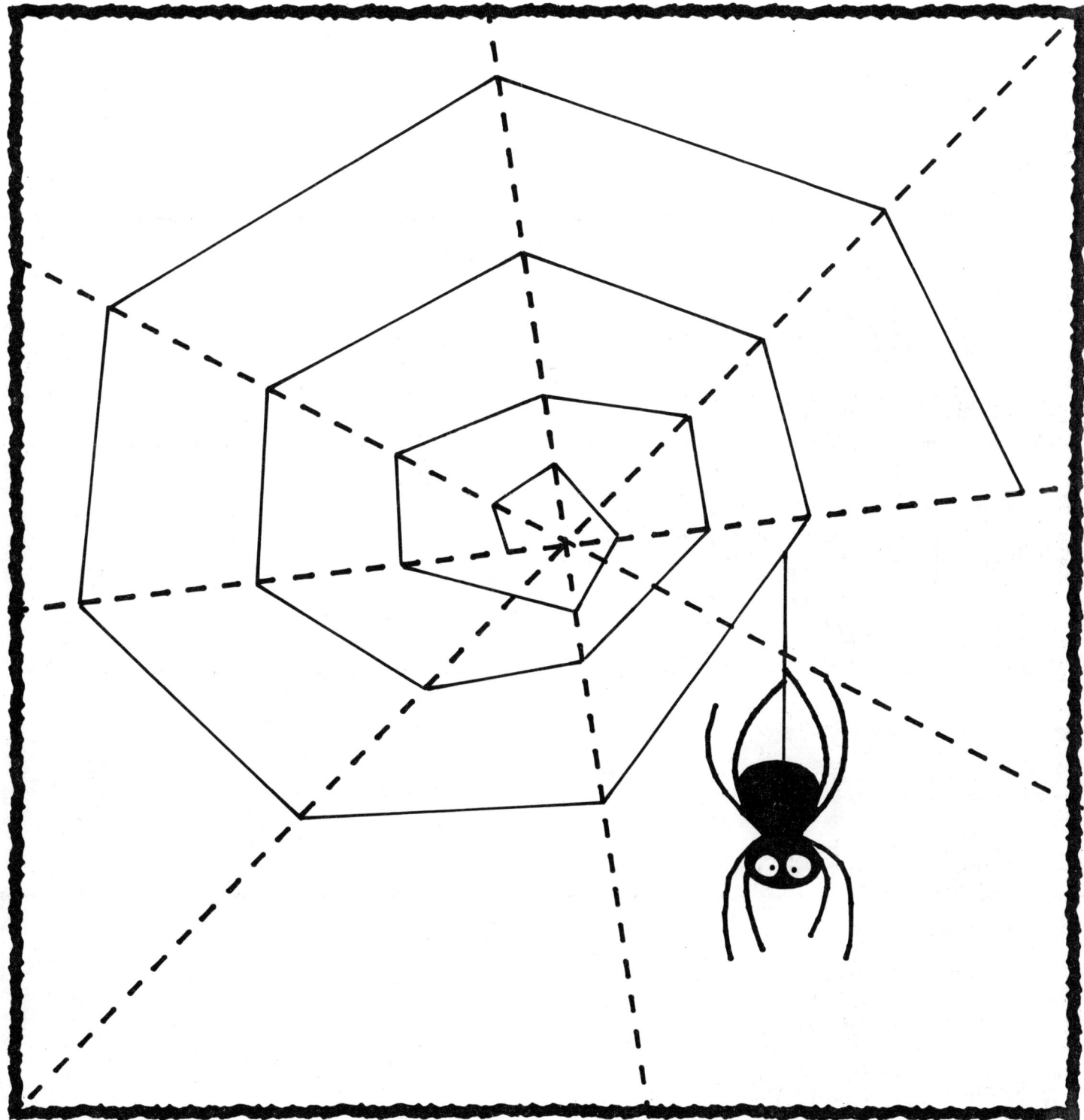

The Preschool Teacher's Pet
©1989–The Learning Works, Inc.

Reading Readiness
Motor Skills

Name _____

Cut it Out

Cut on the dotted lines to make a puzzle.

Reading Readiness
Motor Skills

Name _____

Follow the Line

Connect the pictures by tracing on the lines from left to right.

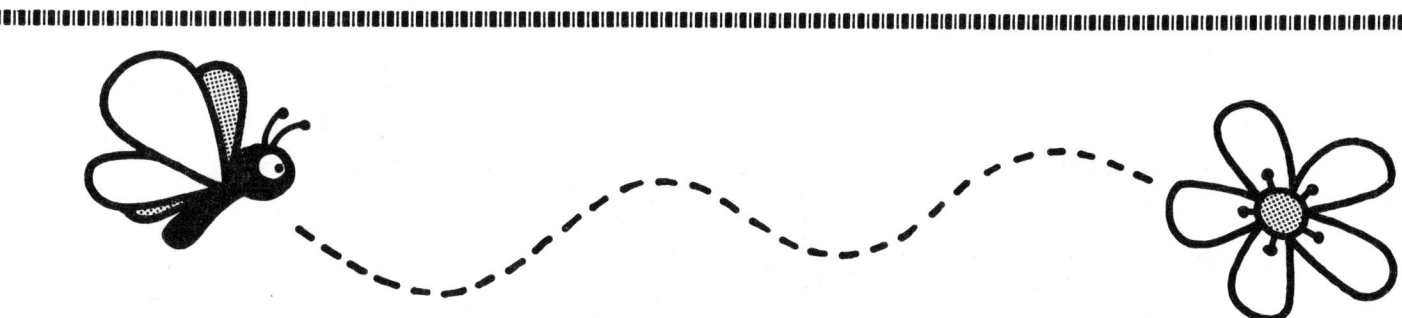

The Preschool Teacher's Pet
©1989–The Learning Works, Inc.

Reading Readiness
Motor Skills

Name _____

Bounce a Ball

Connect the dotted lines and color the balls.

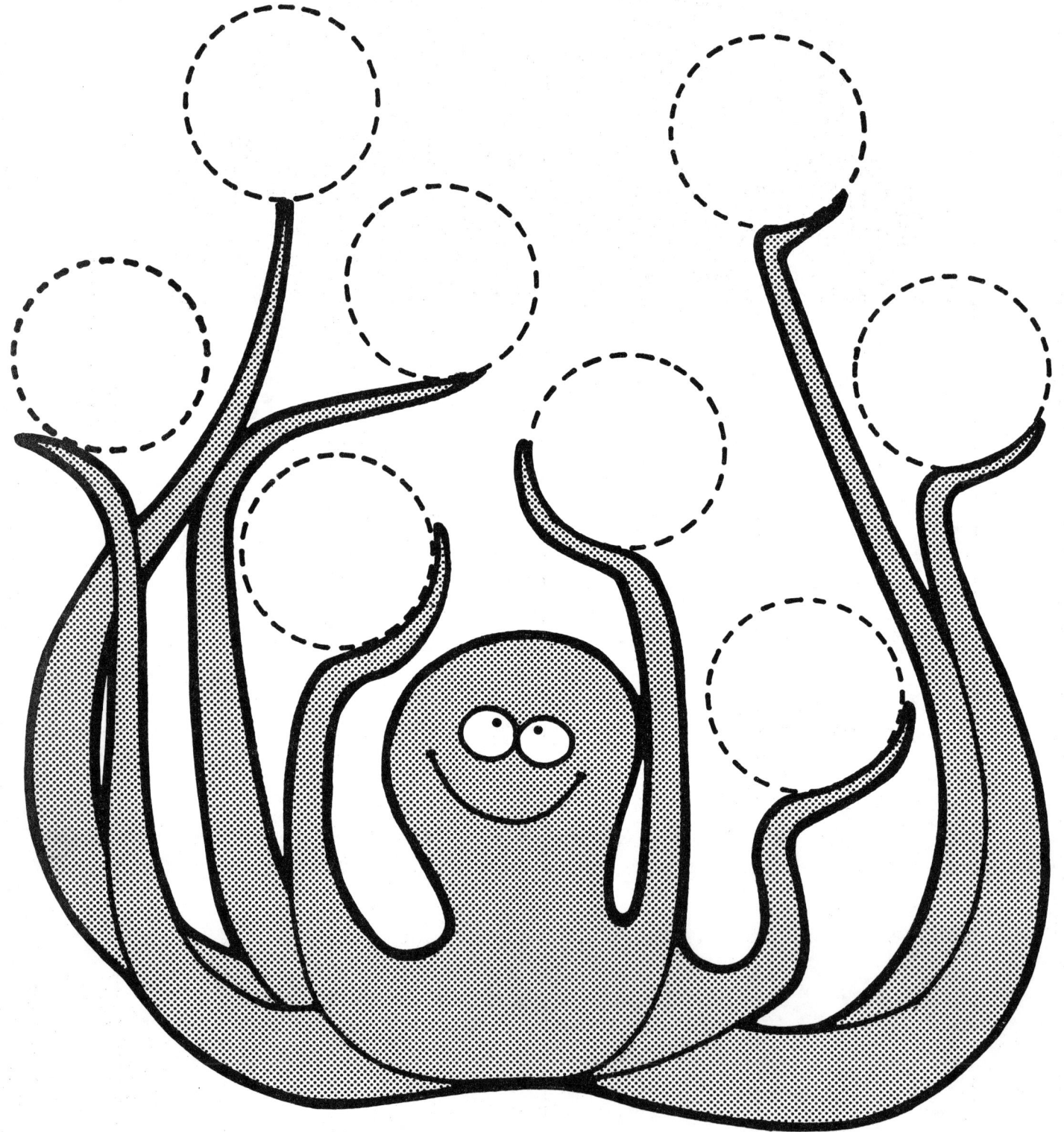

Reading Readiness
Motor Skills

Name _____

Quilt Squares

Complete and color the squares on the quilt.

Reading Readiness
Motor Skills

Name _____

Pizza Pies

Complete and color the pizza pies.

Reading Readiness
Motor Skills

Name _____

Dinosaur Time

Cut and paste the puzzle pieces to make a dinosaur.

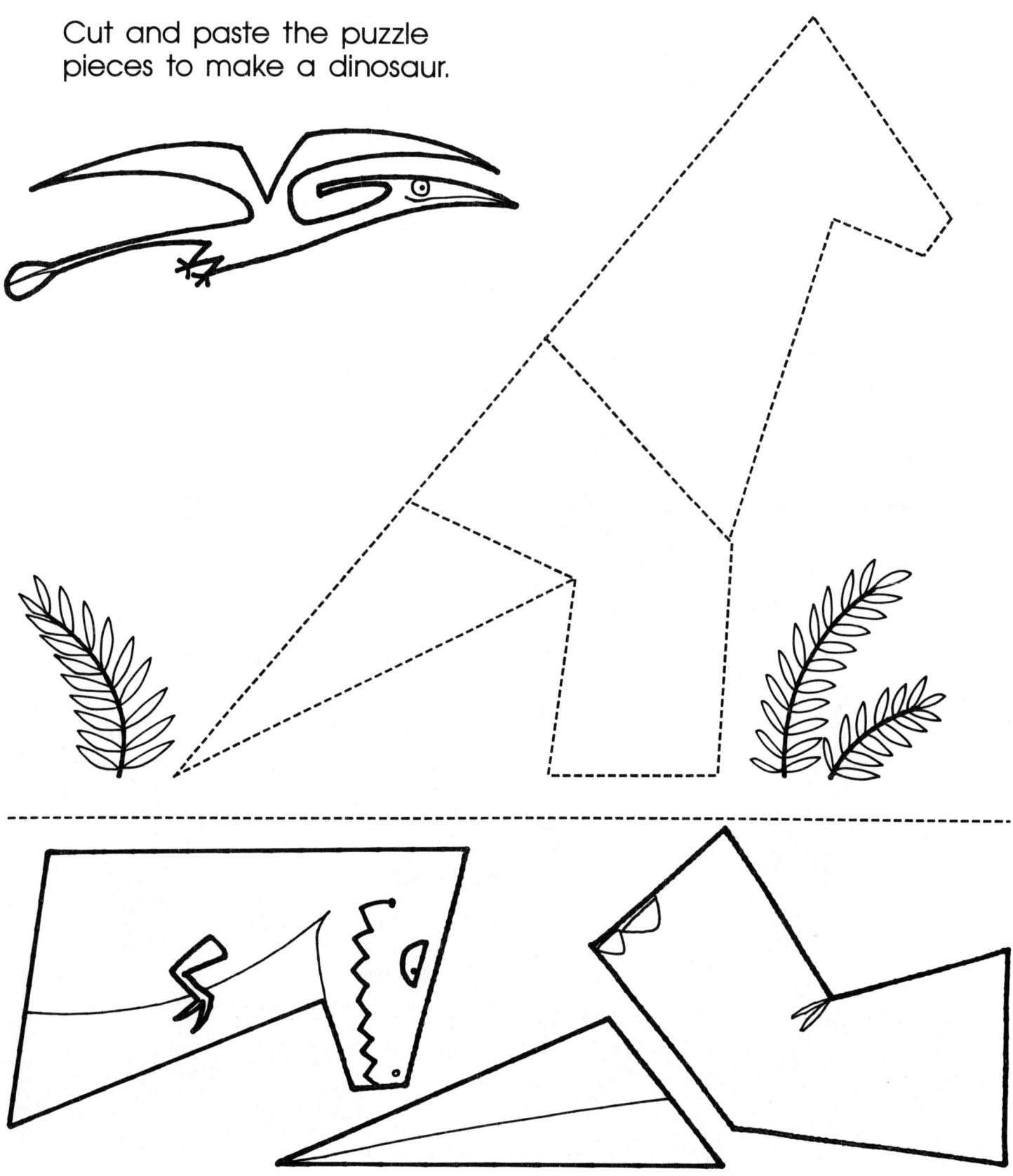

Reading Readiness
Motor Skills

Name _____

Connect a Clown

The Preschool Teacher's Pet
©1989–The Learning Works, Inc.
190

Reading Readiness
Motor Skills

Name _____

Busy Bee

With a pencil or crayon, follow the dotted line from the bee to the flower.

Reading Readiness
Motor Skills

Name _____

Nice Mice

Use a pencil or crayon to draw along the tail of each mouse.

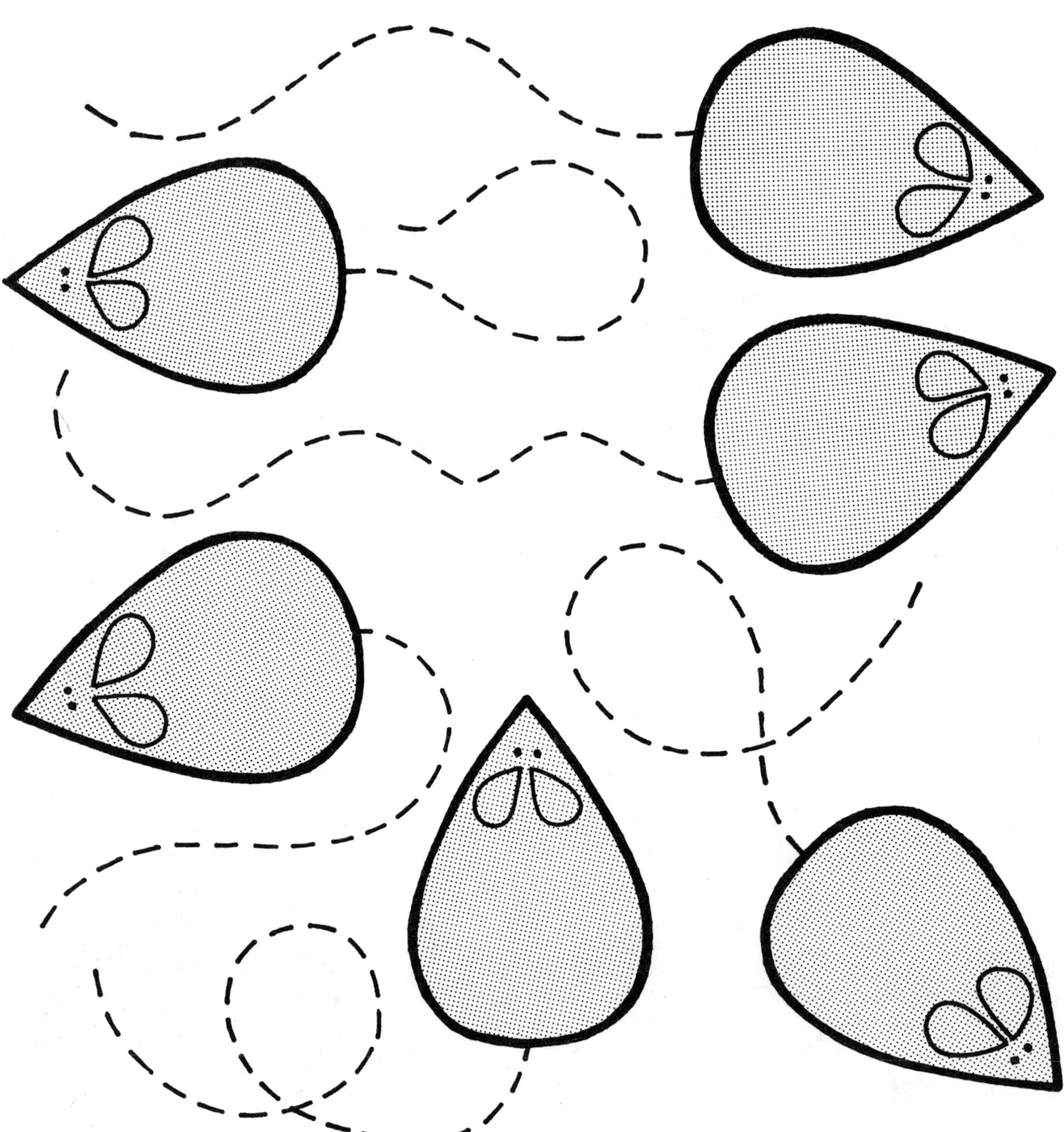

The Preschool Teacher's Pet
©1989—The Learning Works, Inc.